THE CLOSED DOOR
AND OTHER STORIES

Persephone Book N°74
Published by Persephone Books Ltd 2007

Reprinted 2010

'The Closed Door' appeared in *On Approval* (1935) and
was reprinted in *Wednesday* (1961). The next five stories
are taken from *After Tea* (1941) and the remaining four
from *Wednesday*.

Endpapers taken from a 1930s
dress fabric in a private collection

Typeset in ITC Baskerville by Keystroke,
Tettenhall, Wolverhampton

Printed and bound in Germany by
GGP Media GmbH, Poessneck

on Munken Premium (FSC approved)

ISBN 978 1 903155 646

Persephone Books Ltd
59 Lamb's Conduit Street
London WC1N 3NB
020 7242 9292

www.persephonebooks.co.uk

THE CLOSED DOOR
AND OTHER STORIES

by

DOROTHY WHIPPLE

PERSEPHONE BOOKS
LONDON

CONTENTS

THE CLOSED DOOR

PART ONE

I

Ernest and Alice Hart had not expected or wished for children, and, after ten years of uneventful matrimony, they viewed the birth of a daughter with dismay.

Ernest was forty-four and Alice thirty-five when they became, with reluctance, parents. It was too late, Alice complained bitterly, and Ernest agreed, but less bitterly, because he did not have to prepare bottles, wash napkins or get up in the middle of the night. In fact, when Stella was born, he thought it better to join a club to ensure his peace.

The Harts lived in the Chase, where a double row of solid houses faced each other across a wide grass-bordered walk planted with elm trees. All the trees in the Chase were magnificent, except two at the top, which bore tablets stating that they had been planted in 1850 by two eminent aldermen. For some reason, these trees had never flourished but remained thin and wasted and in strange – some thought humorous – contrast to their magnificent companions.

The grave beauty of the elm-tree walk had attracted Ernest Hart, who had a complacent eye for this sort of thing, to the place. Also, since no traffic was allowed, it was quiet for his writing.

Ernest wrote occasional articles for the local papers. These articles, about nothing in particular, always contained a quotation from Latin or Greek, with the translation following immediately below, for, though Ernest was a learned man, he did not expect learning in his readers. Ernest only wrote when he felt inclined, and he never allowed an article to give him any trouble. There was something wrong with it, he felt, when it did that.

Ernest wrote a little and that was all he did. There was no need for him to do anything else. Alice had a nice income and Ernest lived on it without false pride. He knew she adored him and liked to provide him with everything, so he very kindly let her.

Alice, in spite of her income, was inclined to be mean about money. She economised on everything but Ernest. He might sit, in the good clothes she bought him, by the fire in his study, which was the best room in the house, but she must rush about in a shabby dress – she always wore old clothes indoors – cleaning with Mrs Seddon, the charwoman.

Alice could well afford a maid, but she would not. Maids ate food and used coal and light and soap when they were not working, and Alice did not hold with that. So she had Mrs Seddon in every morning and together they cleaned the old, inconvenient house with passion from cellar to attic. When they paused for a frugal cup of tea in the middle of the morning, and drank it together wherever they happened to be, you could not have told which was the mistress of the house and which the charwoman. The house, after the morning holocaust, was clean, cold and tidy. It had a bleak look everywhere except in Ernest's study. Into this unwelcoming world Stella was born one Sunday in February. From the first she was an inconvenience. Her arrival seemed imminent in the small hours, and Ernest, amazed to find himself called upon to do such a thing, was obliged to leave his warm bed and go out into the cold night for the doctor.

Towards the end of the afternoon, when darkness was returning, he was shown his belated first-born. He removed his pipe to exclaim 'Good God!' at the sight of her; then he went back to his study and his book.

Alice was very ill and did not so much as look at the baby at first. But by and by she recovered sufficiently to sit up in bed and outline her future policy to her visiting husband.

'Now, Ernest,' she said, pushing back her hair and drawing the shawl closer round her shoulders; she wasted no money on boudoir caps and bed jackets for herself, or on muslin and ribbons for the baby. 'I shall begin as I mean to go on. This child has got to fit into our lives from the first. This house isn't being turned upside down by a baby, like the Woods' up above. They've already given up their bedroom for the nursery because the sun comes in there. Isn't it absurd? Painted it pink and blue and put bars across the window; you can see it from here. Our girl – theirs is a girl too – our girl must learn that her parents come first. She must understand that she can't make a nuisance of herself. She shan't annoy you, Ernest,' promised Alice. 'I'll see that she doesn't make any more difference to your life than I can help.'

Ernest received this graciously.

'That's all right, my dear,' he said. 'Dash it all, I'm not made of porcelain that I should be handled with such care. I daresay I shall bear paternity as well as any man.'

He squared his shoulders, dropped his jaw and gazed towards the window for a moment in an attitude. To anyone but Alice he might have seemed foolish, but she looked at him with love as she detailed her plans for his protection. He meanwhile filled his pipe and waited for an opportunity to withdraw to his study to smoke it. He knew how to bring Alice's conversation to an end by looking vague and giving absent-minded replies. So by and by he brought it to an end, kissed her and went downstairs.

Alice took up her book on *The Rearing of Infants* and read in it with a frown. She knew nothing about the business, but was grimly determined to do her duty by the child who slept lightly in the cheap cot beside her.

II

Alice, true to her determination, never neglected the baby, but she made no attempt to disguise the fact that she thought her a great nuisance.

'These endless bottles,' she complained, as she sterilised, mixed, cooled and administered them.

'This everlasting washing,' she complained, as she rubbed and rinsed and hung it out to dry.

She greeted Stella's innocent wakings from sleep with impatience.

'Oh, Lord, there she is again,' she exclaimed at the first tentative coo.

Her ways of dressing and undressing the baby made other mothers wince. Mrs Wood, from higher up the Chase, refused invitations to the Hart nursery because, she told her husband, she could not bear to see a baby handled in such a way.

The baby herself bore her mother's harsh ministrations without protest. She did not seem, happily, to be a sensitive or wistful child. She was large, rosy-cheeked and healthy, and if she did not smile much, she did not cry much either.

Every morning she was put out into the garden in her perambulator while Mrs Seddon and Alice cleaned the house. She lay looking up at the trees until her view was obscured by the descent of her bonnet over her eyes. Then she lay unable to see anything, but already knowing better than to cry. Alice, to allow for growth, always made the bonnets much too big, but Stella never caught up with the bonnets. Before she could grow enough to fit one, it was worn out and another was knitted bigger than ever.

When she began to crawl about the house, she had to keep very quiet. If she became exuberant, her father would seize the excuse to go to his club. Ernest liked the club he had joined; it made a nice change and afforded opportunity for more talk and whisky than he could get at home. But it was sometimes a little difficult to go there. Alice did not like him to leave her. So when Stella made sounds of grief or mirth, her father emerged from the study with an injured expression.

'I can't stand this noise,' he would say, reaching for his hat and coat. 'It is more than flesh and blood can tolerate. Goodbye, my dear.' He kissed Alice on the forehead to imply that he didn't really blame her. 'I will return later.'

And Alice would slap Stella for turning Ernest out.

Stella grew out of her pram, but she spent her fixed hours in the garden just the same. At half-past nine she was put out and until twelve o'clock there she had to stop. The solid front door was closed against her. At twelve o'clock her mother would open it and call her in to food and warmth and companionship. Her long boredom would be ended. The open door became a symbol of relief to Stella, and the closed door meant something like despair.

She was not good at playing by herself. After she had dragged about a little cart filled with stones, she didn't know what to play at. She would stand for a while with the end of the limp string in her hand, then she would chew her gloves, then she would trudge about the paths; finally she would go and press herself against the iron gate and gaze out into the elm-tree walk.

There was not much to see, but sometimes the little girl from up above went past with her mother and they made a great event for Stella. The little girl's name was Lucy Wood, Stella knew, and she had flying hair and wore a bright-red cap and coat. She never walked, but always hopped and skipped. Lucy, it seemed, obscurely to Stella, was always free, while she herself was always behind the gate. Lucy did interesting things, but the most interesting of all, was, in Stella's eyes, the taking out of a dog on a lead. He was a nice woolly kind of dog and needed, apparently, a great deal of management. Lucy was always at it, and Stella, gazing enviously through the gate, could see her tugging at the lead and hear her calling out:

'Come on, Buff. Good dog, now. Don't do that. Be quick! Not that way. This way, Buff, Buff, Buff.'

Stella longed for a dog like Buff to take out on a lead. It was her first conscious longing and it was so fierce that it made her ache. For a long time, she dared not risk asking for a dog. She was nervous of exposing her secret hopes to her parents. Sometimes it was all right; they granted the request and that was wonderful. But other times they refused, and so firmly that she never dared ask again. She never could tell beforehand if what she was going to ask for was the sort of thing to be granted or refused, and that made her afraid to take the risk, because once refused there was no second chance. In the end, however, the longing for a dog like Buff got too much for her. She had to ask her mother.

'Mother, could we have a dog?' she began, blushing with anxiety. 'Could we have a dog like Lucy Wood's . . .'

'A dog,' cried Alice, in such a tone that Stella knew at once that this was one of the doomed requests. 'Good heavens, no! Dogs bring too much dirt into the house. We've quite enough to do cleaning up after you without cleaning up after dogs.'

'Oh, Mother,' said Stella, still trying although she knew it was no good. 'I'd clean up after him. I'd wipe his paws on the mat. I wouldn't let . . .'

'That will do,' said Alice firmly. 'You can't have a dog, so let that drop. And go out into the garden. Haven't I told you not to come into the house until twelve o'clock?'

So Stella had to give up the idea of a dog of her own, and content herself by watching Lucy and Buff through the gate.

In the middle of one winter morning, when the trunks of the elm trees had a thin line of snow on the windward side and the sky was low and grey, Stella's boredom reached a climax. She suddenly couldn't bear it any longer. She had dragged her cart about, she had chewed her gloves until now her fingers ached intolerably with the cold, she had gazed through the gate for what seemed hours without a sight of Lucy or anybody else, and now she couldn't bear it any longer.

She made a rush at the front door, grappled with the slippery brass handle, opened the door, went through it and banged it with a loud triumphant bang from the other side. She had got in. She stood panting with the achievement in the porch.

But the bang brought Alice out of Ernest's study. She thought he was writing in there, but he had slipped out of the house somehow and Alice felt bitter. And now here was her daughter disobeying her and looking at her with defiance.

'How dare you come into the house when I've forbidden it?' asked Alice sharply. 'You stubborn little creature! If you think you can get the better of me, you're very much mistaken. Go out into the garden. Go along. Out with you.'

She opened the door, bundled Stella through, closed it and shot the bolts.

The sound of those bolts terrified Stella. She was locked out. She would never get in. Never get into the house again. But she must! She must. She was frightened. She must get in. She burst into tears and beat the door with her fists.

'Open the door! Open the door! Mother, open the door. Mrs Seddon, Father, open the door!' She implored them all, but no one answered. The door remained solid, impassable, locked.

Her panic grew beyond bounds. She was deserted, abandoned by everybody. She would never get in.

'Open the door,' she sobbed, beating frantically. 'Open the door! Oh, Mother, let me in – please, please let me in! Just for a minute! Mother, let me see you!'

No answer. They were all gone. They had left her.

'Open the door!' she screamed. 'Open the door!'

She was so carried away by panic that she screamed louder than ever when she felt a tug on her coat behind. When she turned in terror the grimace froze on her face and it took her some time to realise that it was Lucy Wood standing there with Buff on his lead.

'You are making a noise,' said Lucy. 'What's the matter?'

Stella spoke with difficulty through swollen lips. 'I can't get in,' she quavered.

'Can't you?' said Lucy, who did not seem to think much about this. 'Well, let's ring the bell.'

Stella sniffed.

'I can't reach it.'

Lucy strained upwards towards the iron handle projecting from the door-post.

'No, neither can I,' she said, cheerfully. 'But I can stand on your cart. You hold Buff a minute.'

Stella took the lead eagerly into her hands. Now she was holding a dog on a lead at last. Lucy balanced herself on the edge of the cart and reached the bell.

'There,' she said, pulling the handle down to its limit and letting it fly back. 'That ought to bring somebody.'

It did. The door flew open and revealed Alice, flushed with anger. Her words were arrested on her lips, however, at the sight of a second child on the steps.

Lucy looked up at her with candour.

'She wants to come in,' she explained.

'Oh,' said Alice, recovering herself. 'She does, does she? And what's that to do with you, I'd like to know. You go home at once, Lucy Wood, and don't come here encouraging Stella in disobedience again. Look at the mess your dog's made on the steps! And Mrs Seddon did them this morning. All that time and money wasted! Go away. Take that dog away at once. And as for you, Stella, you'll get a whipping when I've time to attend to you. You'll stop in the garden until twelve o'clock, so you know. And don't you dare to bang on the door or ring at the bell again.'

She slammed the door and again shot the bolts. It looked, for a moment, as if Stella was going to burst into more tears, but Lucy stopped her.

'Never mind. It'll be twelve o'clock soon, because my mother said so. You can take Buff to the gate, and I'll stop outside until your mother opens the door again, if you like. Come on, bring Buff. Now be a good boy, Buff. Come on. Buff, Buff, Buff!'

And Stella, beguiled, smiled with her swollen lips and called hoarsely in imitation of Lucy:

'Buff, Buff, Buff! Good boy.'

The closed door was temporarily forgotten. It didn't mean anything when Lucy was with her.

Alice was not always harsh with Stella. Her temper depended mainly upon Ernest. When Ernest absented himself, Alice vented her chagrin on Stella. But when Ernest bore her company, Alice was happy and treated Stella with good-humoured tolerance.

Ernest himself, when he felt like it, could create an atmosphere of cosiness as no one else could. The time he chose for the exercise of this talent was usually in the winter after tea. They all sat together in the sitting-room then. During the day this room was dingy, since it looked out upon the backyard. Ernest had the front room for his study. The sitting-room was sombre with dark-green curtains and a dark-green table cloth. The plush on the chairs was red, but the carpet drew the colour scheme together by being both red and green. At night, however, when the gas was lighted and the curtains drawn the room was cheerful.

'Now, Alice,' Ernest would say, disposing himself comfortably in his big chair. 'A little more coal on the fire, I think, and the screen across the door. And I'll have a glass of port, and Stella can have a sweet out of the tin, and you can have whatever you fancy. And then I think the Harts will be pretty cosy, eh, puss?'

Stella, sitting on a low chair between her parents, would nod beamingly in reply. She felt safe and happy at times like this. The door was closed but she was on the right side of it. She turned the leaves of her picture book and was warm with contentment and an obscure gratitude towards her parents for letting everything be comfortable.

It was very pleasant, too, when they all went for walks. Ernest was getting portly. His waistcoat rounded in an increasing hemisphere. So he took his family out from time to time for the sake of his figure, and they walked, up and down the Chase between the elm trees or, sometimes, as a great concession to Stella, went as far as the Park to look at the ducks on the pond. Alice hung on Ernest's arm and Stella trundled in front, tightly done up in gaiters, a scarf and a reefer coat. Alice, feeling happy, would make fun of her daughter.

'She looks like a barrel, doesn't she? Go on with you, you little tub!'

And Stella, delighted to please her parents, would strut and show off a little. Sometimes, however, she overdid it and ruined everything.

When the time came for Stella to go to school, things improved wonderfully, for Lucy Wood went to the same school and she took Stella in charge at once. She saved her from mistakes from the first day when she found her leaning against the playground wall during morning break.

'Hello!' cried Lucy, pausing in her flight across the playground. 'Aren't you playing?'

'I can't keep my galoshes on,' said Stella, trying not to cry.

'What's the matter with them?' Lucy looked down at Stella's feet lost in the galoshes ordered to be worn in the playground. 'Why, you've taken your slippers off,' she cried. 'You've got to put your galoshes on *over* your slippers – you've not got to take your slippers *off*.'

'Oh, haven't I?' said Stella, brightening visibly. 'Oh, I'll go and put them on again, shall I?'

'Yes, and hurry up. We're going to play Relieve and you can be on my side,' shouted Lucy, dashing off.

In a moment Stella was shouting too as she had never shouted in her life before.

Lucy was full of lively schemes. The Adventure League was one of them. It was composed of bold spirits to whose company one was admitted after the performance of a deed of daring. After this deed of daring, witnessed by the members of the league, one was presented with a paper disc painted by Lucy in blue with 'AL' printed on in red. The 'L' was sometimes the wrong way round and looked like a 'J' but that in no way detracted from the importance of the badge, and everyone in the school burned to obtain it.

When Lucy said she must qualify for the League, Stella was both fascinated and appalled. Beneath her stolid exterior, Stella was nervous. Besides, she could not think of a daring deed to do. But Lucy hit upon something.

'You must walk on the tops of the peaked stones in the Chase from one end to the other without falling off,' she pronounced.

'Oh, Lucy,' breathed Stella aghast. 'I *couldn't*.'

The stones bordering the walk were huge, peaked and widely spaced and seemed as inaccessible as any mountain range to Stella.

'Course you can,' said Lucy stoutly. 'I've done it many a time. You can practise on your way home. I'll hold your hand to begin with.'

So Stella practised, her mouth and eyes extended to the full. Whenever she let go Lucy's hand she fell off. She didn't like falling off and was inclined to whimper and remain prone. But Lucy urged her up again.

'Go on, you've got to get brave. Go on. You'll soon do it.'

And Stella, conquering a few more peaks every day, was filled with the joy of achievement. She felt strong and proud and waited with excitement for it to be time to practise again.

At last, she was able to announce that she would attempt the whole range on the following Friday. The members of the Adventure League were to be present as witnesses at the end of afternoon school.

'It's terribly exciting,' cried Lucy. 'It's like crossing the Channel.'

It *was* terribly exciting. Stella could hardly go to sleep at night for thinking of it and often, during meals, she forgot her food and sat with abstracted gaze thinking about Friday, until her mother asked her what on earth was the matter and would she get on with her dinner at once.

Thursday came. Lucy allowed her a glimpse of the badge she had prepared for her. It lay in a match-box, a blue disc with the magic letters 'AL' in red. When she had won this, Stella felt she would not only be recognised as a brave girl, she would *be* a brave girl, and might turn out to be a female Casabianca or somebody like that.

On Thursday afternoon, she was to have a dress rehearsal. It was March, and when school was loosed the sky was a clear primrose yellow and the elm trees in the Chase were black against it. It was an hour of great beauty, but the two children did not notice it. With the light of determination in her eyes and her tongue extended, Stella climbed on to the stones and began her feat of skill and daring. Cautiously, balancing herself, she stepped from one peak to another, while Lucy, like an excited terrier, ran alongside with cries of encouragement.

Stella was doing very well. She had passed the twentieth tree. She was more than half-way, when something made her look up and she saw her mother coming down the walk. She at once fell off her peak. She had often fallen off before, but this time she tore a stocking from knee to ankle and rose tattered and bleeding as her mother reached her.

'Stella! What on earth are you doing? How dare you climb on those stones. Just look at that stocking. I can't mend that. It's ruined. And they were a new pair. You stupid girl! Go straight home at once. And don't dare to climb on the stones again. Do you hear?'

'Oh, Mother,' cried Stella. 'I must do it tomorrow. Just once. Just tomorrow. It's for the Adventure League, isn't it, Lucy? Oh, Mother, it's so important. The girls are coming to watch me. Do, do let me walk on the stones tomorrow! Just once for the last time tomorrow.'

'I never heard such nonsense in my life,' said Alice. 'What on earth are you talking about? Stop pulling at me like that. You heard what I said. I forbid you to walk on those stones again. Lucy, what rubbish is this you have been filling her head with? Upon my word, there's been nothing but trouble since she started playing with you. Whatever this Adventure League is, I absolutely forbid Stella to have anything to do with it. Go home at once, Stella, and stop blubbering in the Chase. You look a perfect sight. Go home and put yourself where no one can see you, for heaven's sake.'

Stella turned away with Lucy's arm about her. She wept so loudly that her mother, pursuing her way down the Chase, kept turning round to call out, 'Be quiet, Stella. Stop that noise, do you hear?'

But Stella could not. Lucy steered her home, proffering what consolation she could.

'Never mind. Never mind, Stella. I daresay I'll be giving up the League soon. I'll be thinking of something else you can join. Don't cry any more. See, Buff's coming.'

That evening after tea, Ernest could not conjure up cosiness in the sitting-room. Stella sat, red-eyed and bowed with disappointment, in her low chair between her parents. Alice frowned as she read a magazine someone had passed on to her. Ernest, who did not like unpleasantness of anyone else's making in the house, tried to persuade it away. He pointed out to Stella, as he sipped his port, that these small happenings must be met with philosophy.

'What you must tell yourself, my dear child is . . .' sip 'that although you were grievously disappointed today, more grievously than the occasion warrants, permit me to say – although you are disappointed today . . .' Ernest had a great habit of beginning again – 'you will be less disappointed tomorrow' sip 'and less disappointed still the day after.' Sip. 'Nothing matters very much in this life, Stella, my child. You are young and do not at present agree with me. But you will. In time you will. Alice, this port is excellent. I congratulate you upon it. Now stop that sniffling, puss, and let's be cosy.'

But Stella continued to be miserable, and Alice to be displeased. So Ernest revenged himself. He rose and said he must go to his club. And when he had gone, Alice broke out again and Stella cried again and things were worse than ever.

On Saturday, however, Lucy asked Stella to tea, and they had a wonderful time painting large, watery and peculiar portraits of each other on sheets of paper pinned to a leaf of the dining-room table, arranged horizontally to form an easel for both of them. During the execution of these seeming masterpieces, they divested themselves of their tunics so that, in gym knickers and white blouses, with their hair bundled up under tam-o'-shanters, they might resemble as closely as possible the French artists Lucy had seen in a picture.

Mrs Wood, when she discovered them, said nothing about the gym knickers or the holes made by the drawing-pins in the table leaf. Stella was amazed by such a mother.

The next time Stella went to tea, Lucy felt an urge to cook. When everyone had left the house, it being Saturday afternoon, the children stole back from their play in the Chase, climbed through a window left open by Lucy, and mixed eggs, butter, flour and currants together hastily and at random in the kitchen. They cooked the exciting mess in the oven. It was just done in time for them to withdraw it as they heard someone coming in at the front door. They scuttered upstairs and shut the cake into a drawer in the nursery. During tea they could see steam curling round the edges of the drawer and were seized with giggles they dared not explain. The cake, when finally they got to it, was strangely tough, but the currants were good.

Alice, in her good humours, invited Lucy to tea at times. But it was not much fun in the Harts' house. The children had to keep very quiet and the sitting-room table, shrouded in chenille, was not the place, Alice said, for jars of painting water. Tea was disappointing too; only bread and butter and uninteresting gooseberry jam, and a dry, plain cake with not a single currant, raisin or cherry by way of relief. Lucy got into Alice's bad books by asking, with a loud sigh:

'Need I eat this cake, please? It makes me feel tired.'

'Stella is never allowed to leave anything she takes on to her plate,' said Alice coldly. 'But you as a visitor must do as you please, I suppose.'

So Lucy did not eat the cake, and Alice thought her extremely ill-behaved.

The friendship between the children was close-knit by constant companionship. Every morning Lucy called for Stella to go to school, and the two small navy-blue figures would emerge with their school-bags from the Harts' gate in rain, shine, snow and wind all the year round.

When there had been rain in the night, the children were sometimes late, because, for some reason or another, after rain there were always a great many weak, white worms stranded on the asphalt path between the trees. Lucy, who seemed to have been born with a passion for helping, couldn't pass a worm without helping it to the grass.

'They want to get to the other side, you see,' she explained.

So she and Stella would dart feverishly about the walk with their washed-out worms dangling from their fingers until the town clock struck nine and sent them flying in alarm to school.

They grew. They went up the school together, Lucy brilliantly, Stella just managing to keep up, spurred, not by a love of learning, but by a determination to keep in the same form as Lucy.

The suède-bound volumes of the classics, exchanged by the girls at Christmas and on birthdays, were mute witnesses of the passing of the years. Like milestones, they stood in Stella's room on a white-painted shelf above her bed. Stella's bedroom was as cold and tidy as the rest of the house. She had been trained in habits of tidiness and economy by her mother from the first. She 'saved' things: her drawers held note-books with nothing written in them, new pencils unsharpened, indiarubbers that had never rubbed out, small unopened bottles of eau-de-Cologne she had had as presents and new handkerchiefs still in their boxes. Stella was made to save her clothes too. She always wore old slippers in the house, and instead of changing into something better in the evening as most people do, Alice and Stella changed into something worse.

Alice was impatient with the friendship between Stella and Lucy; not actively, but chronically impatient. Her disapproval of Lucy dated from the bell-ringing and non-cake-eating incidents, but as the years went on, the disapproval grew. Lucy was too fearless and candid for Alice. Alice demanded unquestioning obedience and no criticism from the young, and she felt, obscurely, that Lucy might in time prevent her from getting these from Stella. But she had done nothing so far except to gibe at the friendship, saying from time to time:

'Oh, you and your Lucy Wood! You'd put that girl before your parents any day, and what you can see in her, I don't know.'

Ernest, too, did not entirely approve of Lucy. Ernest only liked people who admired him, and Lucy, as she grew older, admired him less and less. She didn't like the foolish faces he made, she didn't like his pink, perfectly kept hands. His appearance was pneumatic; he looked by this time, as if he had been blown up too high and might burst at any minute.

He was pompous. He listened to himself talk. When he turned a good sentence, he paused for applause, and if he did not get it, he would say, opening his eyes wide in admiration of himself:

'By Jove, I think that was rather well put, although I say it myself. What do you say, eh, puss?'

Stella would dutifully reply: 'Yes, Father, it was.'

But Lucy would say nothing, and Ernest remembered it against her.

Time went on. The girls turned seventeen. The end of their schooldays approached. Lucy was trying for a scholarship at Newnham and looked to her future with eagerness. Stella looked at hers with something like despair. She didn't know what she was going to do without Lucy. She had begged, with tears, to be allowed to go to Newnham too.

'You could afford it, Mother,' she wept. 'You know you could.'

'I've no intention of affording it, thank you,' said Alice. 'I need you at home. After slaving for you all these years, it's time I had a rest. Besides you should thank God – and me – that you aren't in Lucy Wood's position. You are provided for as long as you live. *You* needn't go out and earn your own living. And you needn't marry the first man that asks you, as many a poor girl has to do to get a roof over her head. You've got a good home, good parents and some time you'll have a good income. So stop that snivelling, Stella, because it's nothing but ingratitude.'

Lucy tried to console her.

'There'll always be the holidays,' she pointed out. 'I shall get long holidays and we'll have a grand time together. And when I'm through I'll get some kind of job where you can join me. You'll be over twenty-one then, so you'll be able to do as you like. I'll be a headmistress and have you as matron or something. It'll be a bit difficult for you to be anything else, because you won't have any qualifications. Or I'll be a barrister, or a doctor, or a writer, and you can live with me and keep the house.'

Lucy was fired by the idea of delivering Stella, the Andromeda of the Chase, from her parents who were, Lucy considered, dragons of the worst order.

When the time came for the Harts' annual holiday by the sea, Stella did not want to go. She did not say so, but she showed no pleasure at the prospect. These holidays with her parents were so dull. She was too shy to make friends with young people of her own age, even if she had frequented the places where they were to be found, which she did not. She trailed at her parents' heels about the piers and promenades, watching other people's fun with envious eyes. She wanted to go less than ever this year, because Lucy would be leaving her in the autumn and Stella wanted to make the most of the time that was left.

Her parents thought she was still moping about not being allowed to go to Newnham. It must be admitted that, when they had crushed her, Alice and Ernest often tried, before long, to restore her by giving her, not what she wanted, but something else. So when Stella, in great trepidation ventured to ask if Lucy could go with them to West Runton, adding hurriedly, 'Paying her own expenses, of course,' Alice and Ernest found themselves moved to consent.

Stella could hardly believe it. She was restored immediately. She was wild with excitement and flew to kiss her parents. She loved them ecstatically for allowing her to have Lucy. What a time they would have! She rushed off at once to lay the project before Lucy and her mother.

Alice and Ernest remained in the sitting-room, looking as if they had let themselves in for more than they had bargained for. But it was done now. They tried to make the best of it. Stella had been a great nuisance last year, they reminded each other. Nothing had pleased her. Alice did not altogether dislike the idea of halving the cost of Stella's room, and as four could be fed almost as cheaply as three, she thought a small profit might be made there as well. Ernest philosophically remarked that a fortnight was soon over, and he supposed that if the Wood child behaved with anything like reasonableness, he could put up with it.

And when Stella came back, radiant, to say that Lucy would come, they resigned themselves to the arrangement.

'You made it clear, I hope, that Lucy must pay for herself?' said Alice.

'Oh, of course,' said Stella. 'She never *dreamt* of anything else.'

She was right. Lucy knew Alice too well for that.

IV

In due course, the Harts and Lucy Wood went to West Runton. Even the journey, ordinarily so long and tiresome, was a pleasure to the girls, because they stood side by side in the corridor looking at the flying country and talking excitedly. And when they arrived and found that the bedroom they were to share was a big attic with windows looking over fields to the sea, they were ecstatic and hugged each other. Alice called them to go for jam and bread and butter and tea, and they bounded downstairs and went to the grocer's.

There was a strong smell of coffee in the shop, and as they stood at the counter they saw, when they looked to the front, cooked ham, barricades of butter, and rounds of cheese, but when they looked behind they could still see, through the open door, the sea shining silver beyond the green cliffs. It was wonderful to be able to see the sea wherever you were. Joy ran in their veins like quicksilver and they kept smiling and putting their hair back and fiddling with their collars, restless with happiness.

After tea, Alice released them and they flew down to the sea, feeling very light in their gingham frocks and sand-shoes.

'Oh, Lucy, isn't it heavenly!' cried Stella, catching at her friend's hand.

The weather was superb, and everything promised well. They were superlatively happy. Their cheeks and noses and bare legs were burnt by the sun. Health and vitality radiated from them. They were out all day long, on the sands, on the grass-topped cliffs, in the woods. They came in only to eat and to go to bed. But at table Stella seemed much more inclined to talk to Lucy than to listen to her father; and she didn't know half the time what her mother was saying and in consequence sometimes brought back the wrong things from the shops, which infuriated Alice.

In fact, Stella was so taken up with Lucy that she behaved almost as if her parents *didn't matter*. Twice when they were out, the girls passed Ernest and Alice without even seeing them. And one day, after they had been to the woods, Lucy said dreamily at tea:

'I think we must have a cottage in these woods when we're old, Stella.'

And Stella, smiling at her friend, said: 'Wouldn't it be lovely?'

When they were old! They were planning for a time when Alice and Ernest would no longer be there! Alice and Ernest could not tolerate the idea of not being there to stop Stella from having a cottage in the woods with Lucy. It enraged them. Lucy, had she known it, was piling up trouble for herself.

At night, when the girls had gone to bed, but not to sleep, since bubbles of laughter floated out of the attic window above and in at the sitting-room window below, Alice and Ernest discussed Lucy at length. Alice was voluble and Ernest weighty, but the point they wished to make was the same: Lucy Wood had a bad influence on Stella.

They did not admit to each other that they were uneasy, disturbed, upheaved by the strong tide of youth washing about them, washing them aside, out of the way. They merely kept on telling each other that Lucy was not a fit companion for Stella, that she was spoiling her.

Alice set out to curb the exuberance of the girls by pinning them down to her errands. She was exacting with Stella, getting at Lucy through Stella. But the girls were at first unruffled. They were so happy, they could put up with Alice. And this annoyed Alice the more. Her power seemed to be gone.

But one afternoon Ernest took a hand.

One of the things Lucy did not like about Ernest was his low opinion of women. When Ernest generalised contemptuously about women, as he often did, Lucy burned with resentment, but tried to control herself for Stella's sake. On the afternoon, however, when the wire came to say she had won her scholarship to Newnham, Lucy was wild with joy and excitement and threw caution to the winds. She babbled about her ambitions. Which should she be, she demanded of Stella, a barrister, a doctor or a writer – since now she could be anything she wanted? Ernest thought it time to hit these absurd aspirations on the head.

'Not so fast, young lady, not so fast,' he said, making himself a neat jam sandwich. 'You cannot even get a degree. You may pass the degree examination – that remains to be seen – but you will never be allowed to put 'BA Cantab' after your name. And why should you? Women are a confounded nuisance at the universities and no one should encourage them to go there. As for you being a barrister, you cannot be a barrister. The Courts, thank God, are not open to women.' (This was in the days before the war.) 'You can become a doctor, I suppose, but who will consult a woman doctor? Certainly not your own sex. And in my opinion, and in the opinion of all men, there is something singularly repulsive about a woman's studying medicine. A woman must entirely lose her self-respect during the process, and certainly no one has any respect for her afterwards. I doubt if you will get a man to marry you after that. As for becoming a writer; firstly I am entirely unaware that you have the least qualification for becoming any such thing, and secondly you can never write anything worth reading because you will never have the necessary experience. Women, my dear Lucy, lead small, restricted lives. Men go out,' said Ernest with swelling port, 'into the world, into the streets, the ships, the factories, the offices, the public houses. No woman can have a man's experience.'

'But she can have a different experience,' said Lucy. 'Why shouldn't her experience be as important?'

'Simply because it is not,' said Ernest, as if that settled the matter.

'You talk as if all men led marvellous lives,' said Lucy. 'But they don't. You don't, for instance. I don't think your life is any more marvellous than mine; yet you are a man.'

Ernest was extremely affronted. In the conversation that night after the girls had gone to bed, he told Alice that he was not going to put up with that sort of thing.

'Sheer insolence,' was his verdict. 'And excessively unbecoming in a young girl. Subversive and dangerous for Stella. It's a pity we ever consented to her coming here, Alice.'

Alice agreed. She herself had a fresh grievance against Lucy. The day before, when they had tea at a café in Sheringham,

Alice said briskly to Lucy: 'Your share of the bill is one and six, Lucy, please.'

Lucy was taken aback. She was getting short of money, and therefore had eaten no cakes at all. She was discomfited at being called upon to pay her share of the cakes the Harts had eaten. She handed over the one and sixpence without comment, but Alice had not liked her hesitation. She had noticed it on a similar occasion before.

The climax came suddenly.

True to her policy of making herself felt by obliging the girls to do what she wanted instead of what they wanted, Alice sent them, one hot morning, to Cromer for fish.

'A walk won't do either of you any harm,' she said. 'You must do something.'

Lucy was beginning to notice that Alice was always driving you on. She couldn't leave you alone.

The girls tramped over the cliffs to Cromer and were so hot when they got there that they unwisely spent some time in having ices. Then they tramped back again and were late. And to make things worse, the fish was wrong. There was too much of it and it was too dear.

'Sheer waste,' said Alice standing over the exposed fillets on the sitting-room table. 'Sheer, disgraceful waste. Stella, I'm tired of this. You simply don't care how you throw my money about. You think you can be as stupid and careless as you like and expect me to pay for all your mistakes.'

'Oh, Mother,' said Stella, in a flat voice. She was crimson with heat and exertion and longed for nothing so much as peace and a drink of water. She made a slight gesture as if to say: 'Need we have all this just now.'

That gesture infuriated Alice. It was the match put to the fire that had been laid stick by stick since the holiday began. Alice blazed.

'Stella, how dare you behave like that? How dare you speak in that tone of voice to your mother? You bring the fish back late and throw Mrs Barnes and everybody out for the rest of the day, and not only that, you bring twice as much as we can eat and I have to pay for it . . . !'

Lucy made a mistake. She said eagerly.

'Let me pay for it, Mrs Hart. It was my fault. There were no small fish; they were all big ones. But do let me pay and then it will be all right.'

'Lucy Wood,' said Alice, in a voice of ice. 'Do you know that is an insult?'

Lucy paled and then blushed.

'I didn't mean it to be, Mrs Hart,' she stammered. 'I'm sorry.'

But this apology did not quench the fire. It was blazing too furiously. Alice was revenging herself and Ernest.

'You spoke to Mr Hart the other day in a most unsuitable manner, Lucy, and now I suppose it is my turn. But we are not going to put up with it. For some time we have wondered if you were a fit companion for Stella and now we are sure that you are not. At the end of the week, Lucy, you can go home.'

The girls stood transfixed, their eyes on Alice. There was a brief, complete silence in the room.

Then Lucy, her cheeks flaming with shame and anger, said breathlessly:

'I'll go now, if you like.'

At that, Stella sprang at her and threw her arms round her. 'Lucy – you can't! Mother, don't let her! Oh, Mother, she's sorry. Lucy, say you're sorry!'

Lucy stood with Stella's arms looped round her neck, looking with burning indignation at Stella's parents.

'But I'm not sorry,' she said. 'If they didn't like my being here why didn't they say so, instead of working up a row about *fish* to get rid of me?'

'Alice,' thundered Ernest, rising suddenly from his chair, 'there must be an end of this . . .'

There was an end. Lucy broke the circle of Stella's arms and rushed from the room. Stella, after one wild look at her parents, burst into tears and rushed after her.

But she could do nothing. She wept, she implored, but Lucy continued to pack. While Stella sobbed on the bed, Lucy folded nightgowns and blouses with furious efficiency, bursting into speech at intervals.

'It's no good, Stella. You can't expect me to knuckle under to your parents as you do. I probably oughtn't to say anything about them, although I don't see why I shouldn't, but for your sake I must say one thing.' She leaned on her suitcase with both hands and said solemnly to the figure on the bed: 'They'll ruin your whole life, if you let them. You can't call your soul your own. This won't make any difference to *me*. I shall be your friend just as I was before . . .'

The attic door opened and Alice came in. Lucy paused and Stella raised her head from the pillow with sudden hope. But Alice, it appeared, had only come to say, after consultation with Ernest, that Lucy must wait until her mother could be informed of her impending return, she must wait until the end of the week.

'No, Mrs Hart,' said Lucy firmly. 'I shall go this afternoon.'

Alice's temper rose again.

'If you go now, Lucy,' she said with drama, 'you shall never enter our house again.'

'Very well, Mrs Hart,' said Lucy.

Alice withdrew to report this last insolence to Ernest and poor Stella broke into a fresh paroxysm of tears.

'It's the end,' she sobbed. 'They'll never let me see you again.'

'You must stand up to them,' said Lucy sternly. 'I shall positively despise you, Stella, if you don't.'

But Stella wept on. She knew her parents and she knew herself. She knew she dared not go out with Lucy when they had forbidden it. She dared not defy them and she dared not deceive them. She wasn't clever enough to deceive; she knew she would give herself away in the end and then the last row would be worse than the first.

In this affair, it was she who suffered. Her parents would not give way and her friend would not give way; between them she was crushed. They were so angry they were almost enjoying themselves, but she suffered. Her parents had got rid of Lucy, which was what they had wanted; they would be satisfied now. Lucy was going to Cambridge, to a new life; she didn't need Stella any more and she would soon forget. It was Stella who suffered.

By the time Stella got back from seeing Lucy off at the station, Alice and Ernest had more or less recovered themselves, and true to their habit, after crushing Stella completely, they tried to restore her.

Alice intercepted her as she was creeping up to the attic.

'Come along now, Stella, tea's ready,' she said.

Stella had to go to the table. She sat between them, her swollen lids lowered, reduced by too much emotion to apathy. They passed food to her, they quite fussed over her.

'See how nice it is,' their behaviour implied, 'to be alone once more without strangers, to be together, just ourselves.'

The Harts, Ernest mutely suggested, were pretty cosy.

In the evening they insisted on taking Stella to the pierrots at Cromer. She was too tired to resist them. She went. She sat desolately with them in the front seats. The strong light from the stage illuminated them; Ernest, portly, rubicund, immaculate in a light-grey suit, with Alice, leaning slightly upon him, her sharpness softened as she laughed at the jokes, and Stella, gazing at the pierrots, but thinking of Lucy. When two tears brimmed over and began to roll down her cheeks, she surreptitiously put up a forefinger to flick them away. But her father saw and when the chocolate-girl approached, he beckoned with dignity and selected a packet of chocolate and laid it benevolently on his daughter's knee.

PART TWO

I

One golden morning in October, Stella, from the staircase window, watched Lucy set out for Cambridge. The cabman, stooping under Lucy's trunk, went first between the elm trees to the small side gates of the Chase. Lucy's mother followed, drawing on her gloves, and a moment later Lucy herself flew after them, the soles of her new shoes showing yellow as she ran towards her new life. Stella thought she had gone. But suddenly she reappeared in the tunnel under the interlocking trees and gazed towards the Harts' house as if it had all at once occurred to her that Stella might be looking out. When she picked out Stella's face at the staircase window, she waved both hands vigorously.

'Goodbye . . .' her voice came faintly through the glass. 'Goodbye.'

Then she was gone again. This time the tunnel under the trees remained empty. Empty for good. Stella stood staring at it, bemused in emptiness. Then her mother called from below and she had to go and wash up the breakfast things.

Now that Stella was at home, Alice had cut Mrs Seddon's help down to three days a week. So that Stella by this time was dreadfully familiar with the back-kitchen sink. The sink was like an old stone trough, so low that Stella had to bend almost double to reach it. One corner was stained blue by the blue-bag that was always kept there; the opposite corner was stained brown by the tea perpetually emptied into the drainer above it. When Stella looked up from her labours at the sink, she could see nothing but the backyard wall.

She went about silently and heavily, missing Lucy. Her parents were annoyed that she should be so obstinately miserable. They alternately scolded and reproached her, but as this did not bring about an improvement in her spirits, they decided they must find another, but more suitable friend for her. They produced a girl called Beryl Payne, the daughter of one of Alice's acquaintances. This girl had no friends either, and the mothers agreed that it would be nice for their daughters to go about together.

When Beryl arrived by arrangement one Saturday afternoon, Stella's heart sank. Beryl was like her, she thought; but worse. Much worse, she hoped, glancing into the sitting-room mirror where they were both reflected. Stella's idea of beauty was Lucy's fair, slender elegance. Beside Lucy, Stella felt too solid, too highly coloured with her brown hair and pink cheeks. But beside Beryl, she felt almost slender and elegant herself. This did not give her much satisfaction. She would rather have found Beryl more attractive.

Beryl had a heavy figure, a heavy face and unlit eyes. She seldom spoke. Her deepest joy was to play the violin when her family was out of the house. They would not let her play when they were in because the noise was excruciating. But Beryl, when she played, heard something no listener could hear and was happy. It was unfortunate for both girls that Beryl should be as imprisoned in herself as Stella.

Stella sighed when she saw Beryl. But she told herself it was no use expecting anyone to be like Lucy. She accepted Beryl.

She would 'do.' She supposed that she would also 'do' for Beryl. They had no one else, so they might as well put up with each other. In this spirit, they went for long country walks on Saturday afternoons.

Stella accepted her lot as she accepted Beryl. There was nothing else, she supposed. Monday the washing, Tuesday the ironing, Wednesday the bedroom and the silver, Thursday her father's study and the brasses, Friday the hall, the staircase and the sitting-room, Saturday the country walk, and Sunday nothing.

Alice and Ernest were content. Things were even better than they had been before Stella was born. Stella, no longer a source of trouble, was now a source of comfort. She ran about for them.

'My slippers, puss,' Ernest would say.

'Run upstairs and get my thimble. I don't know where it is but you'll find it somewhere about,' Alice would say just as Stella had settled to a book.

'There's somebody at the door, Stella.'

'Go down to the shop and ask why they haven't sent the things yet.'

Stella came in useful a hundred times a day.

Alice and Ernest liked having a daughter about. Ageing people like young life about them; they draw a secret strength from it. It is right that age should draw strength from youth, so long as youth is allowed to replenish its own strength in its own way. But Alice and Ernest did not think of that.

Stella worked in the house, indifferent to all of it but her own room. She attached herself with passion to her own room. There was not one thing of beauty in it; everything was washed out and colourless, and as the room was over the sitting-room, it, too, looked out over the backyard. The position of the furniture could never be changed because when the room was last decorated, now a long time ago, Alice, with her passion for economy, had not renewed the paint and paper behind the wardrobe and the chest of drawers.

'Sheer waste,' she had said. 'Nobody sees behind.'

Stella loved her room. She could be alone there, and the drawers held accumulations of unused things, which she liked to finger and re-arrange: bottles of eau-de-Cologne, tablets of scented soap still in their wrappers, new handkerchiefs, new stockings, rolls of new ribbon. Now that she had a small allowance of her own, she often bought things to add to her store, and long after she was supposed to be in bed, she bent over the drawers arranging her 'things'.

Winter passed in this monotonous fashion. But one Saturday in April something happened.

Stella and Beryl had walked farther than usual. Stella hadn't liked the look of the tea-places in one village and it proved to be a long way to the next.

'This looks all right,' said Stella, halting before a yellow washed cottage where a board hanging over a thick-budded hawthorn hedge announced that 'Teas and Hot Water' could be had within.

'I'm glad you approve of somewhere at last,' said Beryl.

'I'm afraid I've dragged you too far,' said Stella politely. She was always polite to Beryl.

'Could we have tea?' she asked of the little old woman who answered her knock.

'Well, come in then,' said the old woman rather ungraciously. 'I was just going to get my own, but I suppose I'll 'ave to put it off.'

'Oh,' said Stella, taken aback. 'Perhaps we'd better go somewhere else.'

'No, you can come in, now as you're 'ere. What d'you want? Tinned salmon, crab, lobster?'

'Oh, I don't think so . . .' demurred Stella, following the old woman down a crooked passage.

'Eggs then,' snapped the old woman. 'Eggs, brembutter, cakes and jam, will *that* suit you?'

'Yes, thank you,' said Stella. She hadn't wished for such an expensive tea but dared not refuse it.

'Sit yer down then,' said the old woman, throwing open a door. 'You'll have to sit with a young man, but I don't suppose any of you'll mind that.'

She shut the door smartly behind them and left the girls to their fate. They stood where they were, their startled eyes on the young man who sat at the table, eating an egg. They were terrified of the thought of sitting with him. Neither of them had ever sat with a young man before.

'I hope you *don't* mind,' he said laughing. 'Mrs Harrison is what is known as a "character", and characters don't seem to care how they embarrass other people. But you'll get a very good tea, I can tell you that.'

The girls murmured and moved to the table. They sat down and took off their gloves and pulled at their cuffs with such concern that there might have been something indecent in the exhibition of a wrist. Stella suddenly thought of her swallow and blushed. How could she manage to drink tea? Her swallow always sounded so loud in company. But just then the young man took a drink and swallowed so much more loudly than ever Stella did that she was suddenly and intensely relieved. She lifted her head and smiled at him. It struck him that she wasn't so bad after all, and he plunged into conversation in a determined fashion. He always walked ten miles on Saturday, he told them. Did him good after sitting at a desk all week. He was in Jackson & Baines', the accountants' office.

'Oh, my father knows Mr Jackson,' cried Stella.

'Does he? Perhaps I know your father?' fished the young man.

'Do you? Ernest Hart.'

'Oh, is he the writer? I read his articles. Jolly good they are, too. Bit above my head, but I appreciate them all the same. So you're Miss Hart, are you?'

'Yes, and this is Beryl Payne,' said Stella.

'My name's Jimmy Barrett,' said the young man, holding out his hand.

The girls reached out and shook it; then settled back in their chairs. The blush that had risen to Stella's cheeks still glowed there; her eyes shone and she kept smiling.

This was a nice young man. Somehow he reminded her of Lucy. Not by his looks. He was dark and brown and had white uneven teeth and a prominent Adam's apple showing through his hygienically low soft collar. He had a high bumpy brow, which betokened, Stella was sure, a powerful intelligence. But he had the same vitality as Lucy, the same easy ways; he made you feel, as Lucy did, that life was endlessly exciting. He carried you along with him. She smiled at Jimmy Barrett again, and Mrs Harrison brought in the tea.

Stella was glad she had ordered an expensive tea after all, because it took a long time to eat and Jimmy Barrett sat with them. Halfway through tea Stella realised that something had happened to her. She felt light and unburdened, as if someone had relieved her of something heavy that she had been carrying for a long time. The obscure anxiety she always felt at home, so obscure that she did not recognise it, had vanished. She looked round with sudden eagerness to see what it was that made her happy.

The parlour walls were whitewashed, the cloth on the round table was very white, the sunlight coming in at Mrs Harrison's deep little windows was a radiant pale yellow, and the prim-roses in the shallow dish in the middle of the table were a radiant pale yellow too. There was a kind of harmony in everything, thought Stella. And a fresh simplicity. She looked at Jimmy Barrett and her eyes told him that she had suddenly seen something. He didn't know what it was, but he leaned forward with interest. Beryl, munching bread-and-butter rather as a cow chews the cud, stared at them both in heavy wonderment. She hadn't thought that Stella was 'that sort of girl'.

She sat silent while they talked, only remarking finally that if they wanted to get home that night they'd better be going. The girls were going home by train, because Stella had to see to supper, but Jimmy Barrett had to walk to complete his ten miles. He left the cottage with them.

'You won't find a better place for tea than this anywhere,'

he said as they paused to say goodbye outside the hawthorn hedge. 'What about coming again next week?'

Stella's heart leaped. She had been holding on to every minute of this wonderful afternoon, but it had never occurred to her that it could be repeated. It was amazement rather than coquetry that made her hesitate.

'Well . . . we might perhaps . . .' she said, looking uncertainly towards Beryl.

Beryl was a good sort. It had not been much fun for her, but if Stella had enjoyed it, Beryl was willing to repeat it.

'We might,' she said briefly.

'Oh, yer 'ere again, are you?' said Mrs Harrison, opening the door to them the following Saturday. 'Well, I can't say as I'm surprised neither. 'E's 'ere before yer. Go on in. Same as before in t'tea line, I suppose?'

Blushing and indignant Stella hurried into the crooked passage to get away from Mrs Harrison, but when she reached the parlour door she dared not open it. He was there. He was behind it. She stood with her thumb on the latch.

'Go on,' whispered Beryl from behind.

But Stella would still have lingered had not Mrs Harrison suddenly appeared crying:

'What's matter? Not locked y'out, 'as 'e?'

Stella plunged into the room and greeted Jimmy Barrett breathlessly. But once in his company, the same pleasurable recklessness that she used to feel with Lucy again invaded her. She didn't care what coarse remarks Mrs Harrison might make. In fact, they seemed funny.

'I thought I'd wait and have tea with you this time. You pour out, won't you?' said Jimmy, pulling out a chair for her.

Gaily she took her place behind the teacups. Jimmy sat on her left and Beryl on her right. Mrs Harrison brought in the tea. The sunlight came in as before and illuminated them all. Jimmy rattled away as before and Beryl chewed and ruminated. Stella was happy. The fresh air, the exercise after being cooped up in the house all week, Mrs Harrison's home-made bread, the sunshine and simplicity, and above all Jimmy Barrett's company, contributed to her utter well-being. She stretched her arms suddenly and laughed. Then she realised that one shouldn't stretch one's arms and she brought them in with a blush and folded her hands on her knee. She had finished her tea, so she gazed smilingly out of the window. Jimmy was talking to Beryl for the moment.

Suddenly she felt a hand close over her own under the table. Her eyes flew wide; she almost exclaimed aloud. The hand was withdrawn, but in her palm she felt a small, flat object – a folded piece of paper; a note. A deep blush began to rise over her neck, up, up over her cheeks, right to the roots of her hair. She was engulfed in its warm confusion. But Jimmy was talking hard to Beryl, drawing her attention to something outside the window, and the blush slowly receded the way it had come, down from her forehead, from her cheeks, from her neck. She clutched the note, wondering what to do with it.

Jimmy was still engaging Beryl, but his foot gave Stella a gentle kick under the table, and she realised that he wanted her to read the note.

She swallowed visibly. Her fingers fumbled with the paper, unfolded it, spread it out. Leaning back, she directed her eyes to it under the shadow of the table.

'Can you meet me here alone next week?'

Her heart gave a queer fish-like leap. She crushed the note in a panic, fribbling it to pieces with her fingers. She stuffed it surreptitiously into her waistband. Jimmy looked a rapid question at her. She shook her head. He re-engaged Beryl in conversation and gave Stella another gentle kick under the table. He looked at her again, nodding his head to say 'Yes.'

She shook hers to say 'No.' But he wouldn't have it. He kicked her again, and in a second or so, flashed another look at her that insisted: 'Yes.'

This time Stella could not contradict quickly enough. Beryl swung round slowly in suspicion and Stella hastily poured out some tea she did not want.

She was in a turmoil. Her head whirled, her heart beat madly. She didn't know what she was saying or doing. She seemed, to her amazement, to be keeping up appearances in an extraordinary fashion. And Jimmy was smiling with satisfaction.

They parted. Stella went home in a trance. She was committed to meeting a young man alone the following Saturday. Who would have dreamt that such a thing could have happened to her? Meeting a young man. Meeting a young man *alone*.

II

The week went by somehow. At one moment Stella felt as if she were being swept by a current towards a whirlpool, and clutched wildly at anything that would hold her back; at the next moment it seemed as if she had thousands of miles to travel in a very slow cab, and she longed desperately to be able to get out and walk. But both at long last, and far too swiftly, Saturday was brought round, as it were, to her door, and feeling like a thief, feeling watched, she had to set out for Mrs Harrison's.

She hadn't liked telling Beryl she couldn't go out with her this week. She felt Beryl must know why. But she couldn't concern herself much with Beryl's feelings because her own were too clamorous.

'Oh, you've come by yerself this time, 'ave yer?' exclaimed Mrs Harrison, admitting her. 'It's allus the way. They singles theirselves out in a time or two, given chance. Go on in. 'E's waiting.'

This time Stella had no time to hesitate at the parlour door. Jimmy had it open and stood on the threshold.

'Hurray!' he cried softly at the sight of her.

They went into the parlour and shut the door.

It was easier the following week. They didn't go to Mrs Harrison's. Stella said she couldn't face that lady again.

They went to the woods by the river and sat among the bluebells. The day was marked for ever in Stella's calendar because Jimmy's hand sought and held hers for the last quarter of a mile of road before they parted.

During the week at home, she kept singing. She had no tune in her and all she could think of to sing was a school hymn:

'We plough the fields and scatter . . .'

'Oh, Stella, be quiet,' her mother would cry irritably. 'I never heard anyone sing so flat in my life.'

But it would keep breaking out again, over the sink, over the silver cleaning:

> We plough the fields and scatter
> The good seed o'er the land . . .

'Stella!'

'Oh, sorry, Mother . . .

> We plough the fields and scatter . . .

She didn't know what they would think of her if they knew. She didn't know what Beryl was thinking. It was only when she was at home that she wondered what other people would think. When she was with Jimmy, the world seemed completely empty, but for them. The Garden of Eden must have been like that, she thought.

Saturday came at last, and this time Jimmy held her hand for the last three miles of the road home. And when they came to the parting place, he lifted her hand and pressed it closely against the hard wall of his chest. She could feel his heart beating strongly beneath her palm. They stood in the road, looking at each other deeply over their clasped hands, and Stella smiled; a smile that no one else would ever see. It transfigured her. There in the spring dusk was her moment of beauty. She showed briefly what she could be; what she might have been. Then they parted. With no kiss, because Jimmy, though he longed to kiss her, dared not. It was too soon, he feared.

'Come out early next week,' he said. 'Come very early, won't you?'

'I'll try,' promised Stella.

She went home solemn with happiness. This was love. This was the love that she had read about in books, but no one, no one had expressed it. It was like a light. There were no dark corners in her life now; the light shone into them and showed that there was nothing to be frightened of in life. With Jimmy, everything would be easy. Even if it was difficult, it would be easy with him. She was uplifted, profoundly grateful, and she felt tender towards everybody.

She felt tender towards Beryl. How could she have thrown her over like that? It was cruel. She wondered if she could arrange to go out on Sundays with Beryl. But then Jimmy was hinting that they must meet on Sundays too. If only her mother would let her out during the week, she could go out with Beryl. She must do something about Beryl, because the poor girl led such a dreadful life. Beryl led the sort of life Stella herself had led before Jimmy came into it. After Lucy had gone and before Jimmy came, she amended. How she would love to tell Lucy about Jimmy! She would love to tell everybody. She wished she could tell her parents. The only cloud in her sky was the deceit she practised on her parents.

She hated it. They thought she was going out each week with Beryl; and she wasn't. She was lying, really. And this love was too beautiful to be lied about.

Besides, it would be awful if they heard about Jimmy from anyone but her. And they might easily. One never knew; somebody might see them. And why should this love be conducted in a hole-and-corner fashion? She felt brave about it; she had never been brave before, but now, with Jimmy behind her, she felt brave enough for anything.

Her parents, after all, were very good to her. They had given her everything and were sometimes very kind. They had been very unkind about Lucy at West Runton, but she could forgive them for that now. If if hadn't been for that, she would never have met Jimmy. And now that she would soon be leaving her parents for Jimmy she looked back at them tenderly.

How magnificent the elm trees looked this spring! Why hadn't she noticed before what splendid trees they were? And how the birds sang in the early mornings this year! As if they would burst their hearts in ecstasy. She felt like that.

We plough the fields and scatter . . .

A new confidence infused her physical being. Her limbs moved freely, eagerly. She was not so heavy or clumsy. Her hair had more spring and curl, the colour deepened in her eyes and lips. The inner sides of her arms, she noticed, had a sheen like satin. It was strange, she thought, that she had never noticed that before.

She was so happy. There was only one thing; she was

deceiving her parents. When she had told them, there would be nothing wrong anywhere. Everything would be perfect.

She would tell them when the right moment came. She felt she would know the right moment. And on the Thursday evening of that week when she was sitting with them in the sitting-room, she felt suddenly that the moment had come.

'Now!' something said within her.

She was sitting on her low chair between her parents as usual. The incandescent gases were lit. They shed a greenish light over the three Harts as they sat before the hearth from habit; there was no fire in the grate at this time of the year. No fires after April, Alice decreed, except in Ernest's study.

Ernest puffed at his pipe as he read in a small battered volume of Browning's poems. Alice frowned as she scanned the daily paper. Stella looked at them. She was conscious of the sharp division between this moment when they did not know about Jimmy and the next when they would know. Jimmy had not yet burst into their world. She felt she was actually holding him back; she could see him, brown face, high forehead, Adam's apple and all, and she smiled excitedly at him. He was about to be introduced.

She clasped her book over her racing heart. She glanced at the clock. Almost ten. She would soon have to go and get the milk and hot water for her mother and herself. Alice held that milk was too heavy to go to bed on; besides, a great glass of milk was an extravagance, so Alice let it down with hot water. It took the chill off and was cheap. Alice always combined hygiene with economy. Stella wondered whether to tell her parents before she went for the milk or after.

'Now,' urged something within her.

An exalted look came into her eyes. She laid her book down on her knees and leaned across it, speaking softly.

'Mother, I want to tell you something, and you too, Father.'

There was something unusual in her voice, some thrilling quality that made her parents look up at once from their books.

'I didn't tell you before. I'm sorry now I didn't. But I've been going out with Jimmy Barrett. I love him and he loves me, I think. Well, I know, really. It's all so lovely and I want you to know about it; then I shan't feel sneaky any more when I go out with him.'

She finished, smiling in her foolish happiness at her parents.

There was a dead silence. Even Ernest, so ready with words, was bereft of them. He gaped, with Alice, at Stella, as if she had suddenly gone mad.

'Going out with a man!'

Alice got it out at last. She leaned forward and thrust her face at her daughter, the better to realise the astounding creature.

'You! With a man!' she repeated.

Stella smiled radiantly.

'Yes, Mother.'

'When we thought you were with Beryl Payne, do you mean?' asked Alice.

'Yes, but it doesn't matter now, does it? Jimmy is so nice. I'm sure you'll like him. He's in Mr Jackson's office – you know, Jackson & Baines, and he reads all your articles, Father, and admires them awfully. He reads such a lot, Father. I know you'll like him.'

'Not so fast, Stella, please,' said Ernest, beginning to recover himself and getting under weigh. 'I have no intention as yet of liking this young man. Let us hear, please, who and what he is, where you met him and how long you have been behaving in this servant-girl fashion.'

'Oh, Father, it isn't like that at all,' cried Stella eagerly, and burst into explanations.

But they did not accept them. She was like a bright flame and her parents were like frequent and copious doses of cold water. She did not kindle them; they put *her* out.

Poor Stella. She had thought her new courage would carry her through anything, but under the storm of questions and angry comments from her parents, it began to diminish. She went pale. She looked frightened now, not exalted. She clasped both hands over her breast as if her love was there and was threatened. She pleaded with them.

'Oh, Father, don't say that. Mother, it isn't a bit like that. I love Jimmy so much. Oh, Mother, let me tell you . . .'

She began to cry, not covering her face, but openly as she gazed at her angry parents while they hurled words at her, words flying first from one side and then from the other, beating her down.

Then Ernest, having talked himself to a solution of the incredible situation, rose to his full height to announce it.

'I will deal with this young man,' he said, towering over Stella in her low chair. 'I will go to Jackson's office and request an interview with this clerk. I'll let him know his place. The presumptuous puppy! He's after your money, but I suppose you're too vain to see that. He thought he would snap you up quickly before anyone else got the chance. A fool like you, Stella, will always be a prey to this kind of fortune-hunter unless your father looks after you. But I will look after you. I'll finish this young man. A clerk, forsooth!'

Stella had become very still. She stopped crying. Her hands gripped the arms of the chair. Her father must never go to see Jimmy. Never. What would Jimmy think of her if her father went blustering about marriage and presumption. Jimmy had not so much as mentioned marriage or even love. He would think it was she who had presumed. Too much. He would think she had exaggerated the whole affair. He would not only be insulted, but he would think she was the sort of girl who snatched at the slightest pretension to announce that she had caught a man. She burned with shame.

They had only been at the beginning. She ought to have seen that. She ought to have guarded the fragile beginning of love – not pulled it up to show. She had destroyed its chance of life now.

She was a coward again. She was afraid of what Jimmy would think of her; a husband-snatcher, a girl without fineness, who could blurt out what should have been kept secret. She writhed at what he would think of her. And she was afraid of all her father would say to Jimmy. She knew what it would be like; a torrent of words, brutal, preposterous, insulting. Her father would end it if she did not end it herself. She sprang out of her chair.

'Father, you mustn't go. If you go, I'll kill myself. I can't bear it.'

She stood panting before him as if she had been running.

'Stella, you're hysterical,' said Alice, sharply.

'Father,' said Stella, laying a hand on his arm. 'Listen. If you'll promise not to go and see Jimmy, I'll promise never to see him again.'

Ernest was taken aback. His jaw dropped. He had been looking forward to his interview with the clerk. He felt he would be good at it.

Stella shook his arm. Her eyes were compelling.

'Do you agree?' she asked harshly.

'Well . . .' demurred Ernest.

'If I never see him again – that's what you want, isn't it? What other purpose have you in going to Mr Jackson's office?' said Stella.

She looked at her father as she had never looked at him before, levelly, unchildishly. It had its effect.

'Very well,' said Ernest. 'And now I shall be obliged if you will release my arm. Your fingers are uncommonly sharp.'

'Of all the disgraceful, deceitful . . .' Alice began again.

But Stella, turning on her heel, left the room.

Mechanically she went upstairs and to bed. She lay flat on her back, staring into the dark. At eleven o'clock, Ernest shot the bolt on the front door as usual, and Stella, hearing it, clenched her teeth, but continued to lie, without moving, on her back staring into the dark. Towards morning she fell asleep. When the clock struck seven, she got up automatically and went about her work as usual.

She took tea into her parents' room and drew up the blinds, revealing them lying in the big bed. Alice's lips were still pursed in displeasure, but it was wasted, because Stella did not look at her. She went out of the room as if there had been nobody in it. All day she went about in this state of suspension.

'Leave her alone,' said Alice to Ernest. 'She'll get over it. Look how she got over Lucy Wood.'

Night came again and Stella went to bed to lie the night through as before. But all Saturday morning her cheeks burned red and her eyes kept turning to the clock. Her breath came fast as if she had fever. She looked as if something was happening to a self that was not there.

She was not with her parents in the house, she was in the wood watching Jimmy, but unable to speak to him, as if she was in a nightmare. She saw him waiting for her by the willow tree, which had long ago shed a great limb on which they sat. Jimmy whistled and looked through the ranks of the trees for her to come. He glanced frequently at his watch. Then he got up and went through the wood to meet her. But soon he hurried back to the willow in case she had arrived in his absence.

The birds would go on singing and the stream running past his feet. Nothing would care that he became anxious and bewildered. How long would he wait, she wondered? Perhaps he wouldn't wait long. Perhaps, as her father had said, he didn't really care for her, but only for her money.

Her mother had been derisive at the idea of his loving her.

'Don't start thinking every man you come across is in love with you, for heaven's sake! It's very unlikely that any man will fall in love with you. You're such a big, clumsy thing. Don't you ever look at yourself?'

Her mother was cruel like that when she was in a temper.

All Saturday afternoon, Stella's eyes went to the clock. Three o'clock. Four o'clock. Five. Perhaps at any moment Jimmy would come bursting in. He would come to reassure her that he did love her, that her parents were wrong. Perhaps he was on the way now to rescue her. Perhaps she wouldn't have to sit in this room much longer . . .

Six o'clock. The flush began to fade from Stella's cheeks. All warmth seemed to withdraw from her body. When she shivered perceptibly she got up and left the room in case her parents should see. She went to her room and closed the door. Out of the welter of emotions since Thursday night, she realised that she had been expecting Jimmy to come and find out why she had not kept her promise to meet him. But he hadn't come. He was giving her up quite easily. They seemed to be right; perhaps he didn't love her after all.

But on Sunday hope rose again. She must give him time. Perhaps there would be a letter on Monday morning, asking why, reproaching her. But there was no letter on Monday, or on Tuesday either. She waited all week; but there was no letter. Jimmy had let her go without a protest.

She never knew that Ernest had been to Jackson's office after all.

PART THREE

I

Alice and Ernest went on as before; they soon forgot the threatened eruption of Jimmy Barrett into their lives. But something had happened to Stella. During the weeks that followed the episode, she grew up painfully. She came to realise that it was no good depending on her parents any more. She did not trust them. In fact, she profoundly mistrusted them. They had deprived her first of Lucy and then of Jimmy simply because they wanted to. They had never for one moment considered whether Lucy and Jimmy suited *her*. Lucy and Jimmy had not suited them, so they got rid of them. That Stella was left with nothing did not matter to them.

By the time Stella was adult enough to have explained it all to Jimmy Barrett, it was too late. He had gone to the War. She even caught sight of him marching with the Sherwood Foresters to the station. She only saw him once again, years afterwards, when it was more than ever too late.

Stella suffered that summer. She slept badly, she had no appetite and rarely left the house. When Lucy, who had left Cambridge to go into a VAD hospital in London, braved Alice's displeasure and called to say goodbye, she was appalled by Stella's looks.

'What's happened to you?' she asked, her grey eyes wide under her navy-blue regulation mushroom of a hat.

'Oh, I suppose I'm run down.' Stella put back her lank hair with nervous hands and made a smile with pale lips.

'You look awful,' said the candid Lucy.

'Mrs Hart,' she burst out suddenly. 'Couldn't Stella come to the hospital, too? They need help so badly, and they'd be very glad of her. And it would do her good to be doing something . . .'

'Stella is doing plenty here, thank you, Lucy,' said Alice coldly. 'Her first duty is to her parents. I can find plenty for her to do without her gadding off to nurse officers, no matter how attractive they may be.'

Lucy flushed and rose. Mrs Hart was hopeless. She squeezed Stella's unresponsive hand hard as they went through the hall to the front door.

'Poor old girl,' she whispered. 'I wish I could get you out of this.'

'Goodbye, Lucy,' said Stella, kissing her.

She didn't really want to be got out; she felt too ill. Even her mother was struck by her look of illness when she went back to the sitting-room.

'You'd better go and see the doctor,' said Alice in a grudging tone. She was annoyed that Stella should incur the expense of seeing a doctor. She wouldn't eat and she wouldn't go out, so of course she was ill. What else could she expect?

'It's a pity you didn't see our own doctor before he went to the front,' grumbled Alice. 'Goodness knows how much this man will charge.'

'I don't need to go,' said Stella. 'I shall be all right.'

'You'll go,' said Alice, firm in the face of opposition as usual. 'I'm tired of being told you look ill. It sounds as if we ill-treat you or overwork you or something. You ought to have more consideration for your parents than to go about with that long face. You'll go and see the doctor tomorrow.'

The next day Stella made her way to the doctor's towards two o'clock in the afternoon. The thought of putting out her tongue and undoing her blouse to have her heart listened to by a stranger filled her with nervous dread. When she reached Dr Spalding's house, she dared not go in but passed and re-passed several times, trying to screw up her courage.

Dr William Spalding had been in practice for years in the town, but Stella had never seen him. She knew he was a middle-aged bachelor, and that was all.

At last she opened his gate and went up the asphalt path. The front door, unlike the front door at home, was wide open, and as she mounted the steps she looked right into a hall with a polished floor and a brass gong hanging like a great moon and a bowl of flowers standing before a mirror. The hall was more inviting and cheerful than any she had ever looked into. And as she was putting her hand to the bell the doctor himself crossed the hall. He was a big man with grey hair and a fresh complexion. He looked kind. That was the first thing that Stella noticed about him; he looked so kind.

'Good afternoon,' he said cheerfully. 'D'you want to see me? The surgery is really round the other side, but . . .' he looked into Stella's white strained face. 'Come in here and wait. You'll be better in here.'

He took her into a room that seemed all windows and flowers. He asked her name and said he had met her father at the club. He gave her *Punch* to read, and installed her in a big chair by the fire, and then he left her, saying he would be back soon.

Stella sat with *Punch* unopened on her knee, shivering in spite of the warmth of the fire. This was a nice room, she thought, clenching her teeth to stop their chattering, so warm and light and gay with flowers. What a contrast to the sitting-room at home! How lovely to live in a house like this! Why could other people have cheerful places to live in and not she?

The peace and warmth of the room gradually affected her. She stopped shivering and leaned back in the chair. She felt drowsy. 'How nice to sit here,' she thought, 'with no one to bother me. If only I could get away from home, I should be happy. They'll never let me be happy. But I'm happy here – in this room.' She almost went to sleep, imagining what it would be like if this room was hers.

She sat up with a start when the doctor came back.

'Now, let's have a look at you,' he said, sitting down beside her.

He began, in his kind voice, to question her.

'Is there anything worrying you?'

To her horror she found she couldn't answer him. She shook her head, unable to speak. She was deeply ashamed that now after all these weeks and before a stranger, she should want to cry. And if she once began she felt she would never be able to stop. She bit her lip, grimacing like a child, and gazed at him in silence.

'All right,' he said reassuringly. 'No more questions at present. Let's see, are you anaemic?'

He drew down her lower lid and a tear spilled on to his hand.

'Oh, dear,' quavered Stella apologetically. She snatched her handkerchief from her sleeve and made a dab at his hand.

He smiled so broadly and kindly that Stella was reassured. In fact the incident seemed to set her at ease. She bore the examination with less nervousness than she had anticipated.

He took off his spectacles at last and looked at her consideringly. She was suffering from extreme nervous exhaustion – but why? There must be some acute disharmony in her way of living. But she could not tell him what it was. The little he knew of her did not help him much. Her parents were in comfortable circumstances. She was an only child and probably spoilt. He had met her father briefly at the club, and had formed the opinion that Ernest was a comfortable, cheerful, if inert person. Alice he had seen about the town, and she seemed to him competent and energetic, if a trifle sharp. Had this girl had a disastrous love affair? That was probable. In these days, with young men dying in thousands, almost every other girl had a breaking heart.

'I think you must go home and go to bed for at least a week,' he said. 'After that you should take a holiday in cheerful company.'

Stella was aghast.

'Oh, I couldn't. Please don't make me,' she cried. She couldn't bear the idea of stopping in bed for a week, and she couldn't go away with anyone but her parents and they wouldn't go and it wouldn't do any good if they did, she finished incoherently.

'Have you no friends you could go to?' he asked.

'I have no friends,' said Stella.

He did not take her literally. She was strung up and was probably exaggerating things, he thought. But in a case like hers, it was no use forcing her to do what she was set against. He said he would compromise on a tonic, plenty of rest and fresh air.

'I shall want to see how you react to this tonic,' he said. 'Will you come again on Thursday?'

'This is a nice room,' said Stella, turning wistfully at the door. 'You like it, do you?' said the doctor, turning with her. 'My housekeeper, Mrs Hill, is good at flowers, isn't she? In fact, she's good at everything. She looks after me very well.'

Contentment showed in his pleasant face.

'You'd better wait in here on Thursday since you like it so much,' he said, smiling down on Stella. 'I'll tell Mrs Hill to put you in here.'

'Oh, thank you,' Stella felt grateful out of all proportion. She went down the steps feeling unaccountably better than when she went up them.

II

It would be hard to say when the idea that she might marry the doctor took definite shape in Stella's mind. At first, she only felt a strong desire to attach herself to this man who was so kind. She made as many excuses as possible for visiting him and here the doctor's dog, George, was useful. George was a white, woolly terrier very like Lucy's Buff, and when Stella told Dr Spalding how she had longed for a dog to take for walks, the doctor, looking for a way to make his patient take more air and exercise, suggested that she should promenade George. He was too much of a carriage dog, altogether, he said, since he sat in the brougham while his master made his rounds.

So Stella, making it clear to her mother that her visits would not be charged for, called two or three times a week at the doctor's house to take George out and to see the doctor when she brought George back.

She showed her attachment in naïve ways that caused William Spalding much amusement, but no alarm. He was entrenched in bachelordom; at fifty-five he felt entirely safe. He was very comfortably looked after by Mrs Hill and Janet, the maid, and did not feel the least inclination to change any of his ways. So when Stella brought him tablets of scented soap and new pencils, and, later, when her store was exhausted, tins of chocolate biscuits and pots of hyacinths – giving him with some lack of imagination all the things she liked herself – he merely put her down as an affectionate girl with peculiar ways and was unperturbed.

He enjoyed Stella's visits. He was contented and busy, but after his work it was nice to see young life about the house. And he felt protective and indulgent towards Stella as towards a young creature he had nursed back to health.

But it was with a shock, one afternoon in spring, that he realised what he had let himself in for.

He had come in from his afternoon visits to find Stella in the sitting-room with George. Mrs Hill brought in tea and they had it together. Afterwards the doctor lit his pipe and Stella took the chair across the hearth. She kept saying from time to time that she must go, but she stayed.

'Isn't it strange that, in life, we keep reviving?' she said suddenly.

'We're certainly pretty tough,' agreed the doctor, puffing his pipe in contentment.

'I thought I should never revive when I had to give up Jimmy,' she said. She had long ago told her friend about Jimmy. 'But you see, I did. There are different sorts of love, aren't there? They don't say so in novels, but there are. I loved Jimmy one way, but I love you, for instance, in another.'

He smiled indulgently.

'Thank you, my dear, that's very charming of you.'

'But I mean it,' said Stella gravely.

He smiled again.

'I hope you don't think it's sort of bold of me to say that?' said Stella anxiously.

'No, of course not,' said the doctor. 'We're friends by this time, I hope. You can say what you like to me without being afraid that I shall misunderstand you.'

'Can I really,' asked Stella eagerly.

'Of course.' He puffed away, unaware of what approached.

'Well, then,' said Stella, leaning forward. 'I think you're the kindest man I ever saw. You're my ideal.'

'Heaven forbid!' said the doctor, feeling the first prick of apprehension. 'There's nothing ideal about me. Spare my blushes!'

'I suppose you think I'm silly,' said Stella.

'No,' he reassured her. 'You're young and generous, that's what it is.'

'You don't feel I'm thrusting my affection on you, do you?' persisted Stella.

'Not at all. I'm very fond of you too, as you know.'

'Are you?' Stella's voice took on a sudden light note. 'Are you really?'

'Of course I am.'

'Oh, do you mean that?' To his amazement, she slid from her chair to the rug at his feet and knelt there, looking up at him beseechingly. 'Do you really love me? Do you? Oh, I love you. You're so kind and I'm so happy when I'm with you.'

'My dear child,' he exclaimed. 'Do get up. And don't talk so wildly.'

'It isn't wild,' said Stella, laying her cheek against his knee. 'It's true. I love you.'

'No, of course, you don't. You like me, you mean. I'm an old man. I'm fifty-five,' he protested, trying to lift her from the floor by her elbows. But she was too heavy for him and she resisted.

'Fifty-five's not old,' she said. 'It's no age at all.'

'That's very kind of you,' he said. 'But I insist that I'm an old man. Now get up and be a sensible girl, Stella.'

'Now you've called me by my name. I've been wanting that so much. Didn't you mean it when you said you were fond of me?' she asked imploringly.

'Yes, of course I did. I am fond of you,' said the doctor.

'I've been so unhappy,' said Stella, laying her cheek again upon his knee. 'And you've made me so happy lately. You've changed all my life.'

He was touched. He didn't wish to be touched, but he was touched. His heart was too kind. Pity got the better of caution. The outline of her cheek against his knee was pitiful and child-like. He laid his hand on her hair. Pretty hair it was; thick and soft under his hand.

'My dear Stella,' he said gently. 'You mustn't waste your love on an old man like me. You must save it for a young man, like Jimmy.'

'No,' said Stella. 'That's all over. I've changed now. I could only love you.'

'You can't mean this,' protested the doctor.

'I do. I do,' repeated Stella.

She clung to him. There was a silence. Over her head William Spalding sent bewildered glances round the room, at his past, at his future. He was very well as he was; he had his work, his comfortable house, his good housekeeper. If he married, everything would be changed. A wife, children – he thought incoherently – what an upheaval! Young life in the house! Could he cope with it? Did he want to? No, he didn't. But that feeling of being out of life – of not being included anywhere? It didn't often trouble him – but still . . . And this young thing attaching herself to him! It was pathetic. It was his own fault. He should have seen it coming. All those tablets of soap . . . those chocolate biscuits . . . his thoughts whirled.

Stella moved, so that her chin rested on his knee and her eyes, in which the tears stood, fixed on his face with an expression of appeal and dependence that reminded him of his dog George. He laughed ruefully. She was endearing. She was young, pitiful. She was too much for his warm heart. Stifling a sigh, he bent down and kissed her.

Stella went home in triumph. Now she would tell them something they could not do anything about. William was nearly as old as they were. He was in a settled position. Better than theirs probably. They wouldn't be able to frighten him off, or threaten her. He was as powerful as they were.

She waited until after supper, when they were seated, as usual, in three chairs before the empty grate, for it was April again. She told them and waited, with the pleasurable anticipation, for the storm. But it did not come. Taking off their spectacles, they remarked mildly that they were not surprised. They had seen it coming, they said, and on the whole Stella had done very well for herself. Ernest announced himself willing to receive William on the morrow, and Alice said he must stay to supper. They must get four-pennyworth of cream from the milkman in the morning. Stella must not forget.

'I suppose I shall have to have Mrs Seddon in every morning when you're married,' remarked Alice.

Stella went to bed feeling rather flat.

III

But in June she was married to William and now at last she was happy. Not ecstatically happy as she might have been with Jimmy, but very contented and comfortable. William was so kind. Mrs Hill, at Stella's request, had stayed on, and marriage for Stella was like a long holiday in a particularly good hotel where one wore one's best clothes all the time and never knew what was coming to table. She was secretly amazed that there should be cream with the porridge every morning and cake for tea *every* day. Sometimes she was pricked by a slight fear that they could not possibly go on thus without being ruined; but they did go on, and they were not, presumably, ruined.

She was now her own mistress. She could do as she liked, and one of the first things she did was to write and ask Lucy to come to stay. But Lucy wrote back to say she was being married in London that very week to an officer she had nursed, and who was now demobilised.

'A war marriage,' said Stella gravely. 'But Lucy was always one to take risks.'

She herself hated risks. She was thankful to be safe with her kind William, out of reach of she didn't quite know what. She had been brought up not to expect much from life, so that what she got from it now seemed splendid.

She visited her parents two or three times a week. She shopped for them, and would set and make meals for them. She did as much as possible while she was in their house so as to make it all right to get away. As soon as she had done all she could for them, she said goodbye, banged the front door – which used to be a source of such anguish to her – and although she was a married woman and wore a spotted veil at times, she took to her heels and ran down the elm tree walk, so glad was she to be leaving that dull, cold, shabby house and to be going back to her own home in Broad Street.

A year had gone by, but it seemed to be no time at all, before Lucy wrote to ask Stella to be god-mother to her baby girl.

'Do be quick and have a baby,' she wrote. 'They are such darlings and we could compare notes.'

Stella sent a silver mug and congratulations, but she did not say anything about having a baby of her own. She was afraid of having children. William remarked from time to time that he was not getting any younger and that he would like to see their child grow up, but he was patient with Stella's fears. He was secretly rather baffled by his young wife. She had undercurrents of fear and repression that he could not account for. He was not a profound psychologist, and he was rather apt to think that kindness solves all human problems, but of course it does not.

He was right, however, in thinking that Stella was improving. She was responding to happiness, expanding, growing. She was learning to be active instead of merely passive. She was learning to give. In the house in the Chase there had been no giving. Alice would never part with anything for nothing. If she passed on old clothes to Mrs Seddon, she exacted payment in work.

'I'll give you this pair of Mr Hart's trousers and then you can spring-clean the bedroom,' she would bargain.

But William gave endlessly, publicly and privately. To his poor patients he gave his services, medicine, money, help of all kinds, and Stella was beginning to look on life from a different angle and to experience a new kind of happiness in helping too, although she felt rather self-conscious about it for a long time.

It seemed as if all was set fair for Stella. But one foggy night, in the third year of her marriage, Ernest Hart was killed on his way home from the club by one of the motor-cars that now overran the streets of the town.

Alice's grief was terrible. It was so savage and strident that Stella was appalled. Alice would neither eat nor sleep; she would scarcely even wash or comb her hair. Day after day and often night after night, Stella sat helplessly by while her mother ranged the house, calling out in her harsh voice all her bitterness and love.

William Spalding said it could not go on. There was nothing for it but to bring Alice to live with them.

Stella went pale when he said this.

'Don't, William,' she said, gripping the sides of the table where she sat. 'Please don't bring Mother to live here. I'll go every day as long as she needs me. I'll stop every night. But don't ask her to live with us.'

'But Stella, it's inhuman,' protested the kind William. 'We can't possibly leave her where she is. There's nothing for it but to have her here. In her state she might kill herself and then what would you feel?'

Stella fought hard for her happiness. But she was beaten. William and the circumstances beat her. Alice came to live in Broad Street.

At first Alice took no notice of anything in the house. She was lost in grief. But gradually the change of scene, the doctor's care and Mrs Hill's excellent fare began to have their effect. They did her good. Alice was restored to herself. She began to dominate the household.

'Stella, you ought to be ashamed to let Mrs Hill manage your house. Why don't you manage it yourself. Why do you allow her to serve roast meat every day, for example?'

'Because William won't eat stews,' said Stella shortly.

'That's because the stews are badly made, then. I don't think you ought to sit in that good skirt either. I shall ask William to let me see Mrs Hill's accounts – in his own interest. Just look at the hairs that dog has left on the rug. White hairs all over the place. It's disgusting.'

Before Alice had been in the house two months Mrs Hill gave notice. And at the end of the third she went, and most of the comfort of the house went with her.

Alice said they could manage very well with Janet. But Janet could not manage with Alice. After an outburst which William himself was called in to quell, Janet followed Mrs Hill, and Alice said they must get in Mrs Seddon 'for the time being'.

The house in Broad Street began to take on the look of the house in the Chase. The front door was kept closed. Alice said the patients must not be encouraged to trail up the steps. They must go round to the proper door. The dog made quite enough work she said. Poor George's life was now a misery. At the very sight of Alice, he dropped his tail and slunk out of the way.

There was no longer a fire in the waiting-room to hearten the patients who sat round the walls there. Fires made work, said Alice, and were unnecessary because there were so many people in the waiting-room that they kept each other warm. She did not notice that after a time there were not so many.

People began to think there was something queer going on. Why had the good housekeeper left? And the smart maid?

Why were there no flowers about now? And why were there holes and darns in the window curtains? Why, when you rang the house bell, was it answered by the doctor's wife herself, and so shabbily dressed too, and why, if you chanced to look behind her, was her mother dressed more shabbily still? Even the poor old lady had to work like a servant, they told each other, discussing things in low tones as they walked to the doctor's gate, clutching their white-papered bottles of medicine.

'Funny, isn't it?' they would remark, casting surreptitious backward glances at the house.

And gradually they went somewhere less funny. They were poor and they often didn't pay, so Alice let them go with scorn. William was better without such patients, she said. They made a lot of work, and William didn't seem up to it now.

William was not the man he used to be. He felt his sixty years more than he should have done. He was always tired, and though he tried to rest as much as possible, he could not draw the old contentment from his pipe and his paper, because Alice and Stella were always quarrelling near by. He could not get away from the ugly sound of quarrel.

William had been happy as long as things went smoothly in his life; when things went badly he was not happy at all. For that matter, most of us are like that. He bore Stella a grudge that she could not manage better for him. She was not a child now; she was nearly thirty. She ought to have been able to manage better, he felt.

But Stella bore him a deeper grudge because he had brought her mother to live with them. He was kind, yes, but he should have been kind to his wife in preference to his mother-in-law. Stella had given all up as soon as her mother had come into the house. She knew how it would be; and it was.

And so this disintegrated household drifted on, and in the eighth year of his marriage, William took influenza and died without reluctance. Life had become too unpleasant for him to wish to continue it. He died, the victim, not of influenza, but of his own kindness.

One thinks, romantically, that women to be fatal must be beautiful like Helen of Troy or the Egyptian Cleopatra; but plain, harsh, mean women like Alice Hart are fatal. They destroy as surely, but without the ecstasy that perhaps makes the ultimate destruction worth while. Poor William died of Alice. But poor Stella had to go on living with her, which was perhaps the worse fate.

William did not leave much money. No wonder, said Alice, living at the rate he did in Mrs Hill's day. There would have been still less, she pointed out, if she hadn't come in time to save some for him.

The house in Broad Street was sold with the practice, and Stella went back with her mother to the house in the Chase, which had remained empty after its last let.

'Back again,' thought Stella, going about the familiar rooms. 'There's no escape.'

Alice had brought her furniture out of store, and everything in the house was much as it had been before, except that Stella had collected her best furniture and silver into the room that had been Ernest's study and locked the door on them. Once a week, she shut herself in and cleaned everything with passion.

She had more 'things' than she used to have; that seemed to be the only difference in her life.

Until she was within a few days of her fortieth birthday, Stella remained in bondage to her mother. Then Alice, in her turn, died and Stella was free at last. But it was too late, she told herself.

V

Outside it was a bright March day. There was a surging in the tops of the elm trees that sounded like the sea, and dazzlingly white clouds sailed like ships in the blue sky. It was a day that invited you to go out with a child or a dog, but Stella glanced indifferently through the front windows and went to sit in the room that looked out on to the backyard. She sat there from habit and had not the impulse or the power to free herself.

She was alone in the house. Mrs Seddon had gone home. Stella had lunched on a boiled egg and a cup of tea, and now she thought she would have a nap. Afterwards she might read for a while. She wished she had changed her book this week, but she didn't like going to the library. She didn't like meeting people. She couldn't find anything to say to them somehow. She would read the book she had, although she wasn't enjoying it much. Then she would have tea and do some mending and go to bed early. Today would be just like yesterday and tomorrow just like today. But she didn't mind about that any longer.

She folded her hands on her knee and composed herself for one of her uneasy naps. But suddenly there came a loud jangle at the front doorbell, which made her eyes fly open and her heart beat fast.

'Who can it be?' she said, leaping to her feet.

The house was so unvisited that a ring at the bell threw her into confusion. She stood in the middle of the room.

'I'll pretend I'm out,' she said. 'And then they'll go away.'

But the bell jangled again. The outraged wires twanged in the walls.

'Who can it be, ringing like that?' thought Stella with irritation.

She tiptoed into the front room and peered through the curtains. She found herself looking at the back of an elegantly dressed woman who stood on the step and held one gloved hand to the bell as if she were going to ring again in a moment. She did, with determination; and as she rang she turned round. Stella gasped. It was Lucy! In her amazement Stella pulled aside the curtain and Lucy saw her.

'Here!' cried Lucy, laughing. 'Why don't you let me in?'

Stella dropped the curtain and moved with reluctance to the door.

'Fancy looking at me through the window,' said Lucy, kissing Stella warmly.

'I didn't know you at first,' stammered Stella.

'I'm fatter, I know,' admitted Lucy, going into the sitting-room, 'since Timothy was born.'

'Have you got *another* baby?' asked Stella in amazement.

'Yes. Four now. And all thriving and all looking forward to their Aunt Stella,' said Lucy sitting down.

'What do you mean?' asked Stella.

'I've come to fetch you, my love. You must please come and live with us. We've got plenty of room, and Richard is more than willing.'

'Lucy!' cried Stella, sinking down into the old low chair.

'Yes. I know it's sudden. But I wouldn't risk writing. I knew you'd make all sorts of excuses and say no. So I came. And I want you to pack a few things and come back at once with me, because I can't leave the children long. You can come back here later when you've settled with us and close up this house for good. So come along, Stella darling, and let's begin to get off.'

She smiled her old persuasive smile at Stella, but Stella did not respond.

'You are very kind,' she said, mutely pushing Lucy off. 'But I can't accept your invitation.'

'Oh, Stella, don't be stiff with me. You must come, please. I want you so much.'

'It's very kind of you,' said Stella again. 'But I can't.'

'Oh, why?' cried Lucy.

'Because I would rather stay here,' said Stella.

'Stella, you can't possibly want to stay here! Alone, in this dingy old house! Why, it's a dreadful place, and you know it.'

'I'm used to it,' said Stella stubbornly. 'I can't change my ways now. I'm too set in them. I can't leave my things. You can't ask me to get up and walk out of the life I'm used to at a moment's notice, Lucy. And at my age, too!'

'I'm asking you to come and stay with us for a while, and if you like us, to stay with us. But if you want to come back, you can,' said Lucy. 'And what's your age? It's my age, too, isn't it?'

They argued in the back room. Lucy with growing impatience, Stella with stubborn perversity, clinging to her old life like a drowning man resisting rescue from his straw. As she talked, Stella was noticing that Lucy looked years younger than she did. She marvelled that Lucy's face was still unlined, her hair as bright as ever, her eyes as unclouded. Lucy looked shiningly happy, in spite of her impatience, and Stella beside her felt so shabby, tired and spiritless that she wished Lucy would go, so that she would not be faced with this contrast any longer.

But Lucy persisted. It was not until Stella made a dreadful remark about not being able to stand children that Lucy gave up.

'Children make such a noise,' said Stella wearily, putting her hand to her head. 'I couldn't stand children now.'

'Very well,' said Lucy, hurt at last. 'You must stay here, I suppose. I'm sorry I troubled you. I'll go now and catch the earlier train. Goodbye, Stella. I'm very disappointed.'

Stella took her to the door and before Lucy had reached the bottom step, she closed and bolted it upon her. She rushed back to the sitting-room and threw herself into the chair. Her face grimaced uncontrollably, her breast rose in a great sob.

Fool! Fool that she was! She had shut herself in. Shut herself in for ever. No one would ever try to get her out again now. She had sent her only friend away. She would probably never see her again. And life was so long. What could she do with her long, empty life? She rocked herself backwards and forwards in her chair, weeping into her hands.

There was a loud ring at the front door, followed by a violent rapping on the wood. Then a voice called urgently through the letter-box:

'Stella, let me in! Stella! I'm not going home without you, so now you know. You'd better let me in before the police come to see what's the matter. Stella! I can't ring and bang here as I did that long time ago without being taken up as drunk and disorderly. Stella, hurry up! Open the door!'

Stella listened for a moment, with the tears stuck on her cheeks, a light dawning in her eyes, then she plunged into the hall, banging herself against the walls in her haste. She drew the bolts and Lucy burst into the house.

'There – you goose! You see! You wanted to come after all,' she cried triumphantly, throwing her arms round Stella so that her handbag dangled grotesquely against Stella's agitated back. 'What a blessing I came back! And I nearly didn't. Come on, love, we can cry in the train. Let's get to the packing.'

'Oh, Lucy,' laughed Stella, wiping her eyes and scrambling upstairs after her friend. 'You haven't changed a bit.'

'No,' admitted Lucy cheerfully, 'I haven't. All my life I've wanted to get you out of here, and now I'm going to do it. Be quick. We must be on the right side of that door in three-quarters of an hour at the latest.'

THE ROSE

Pausing at an upstairs window, Elsie Smith watched her husband go down the garden path. She thought he had left for the office long ago, but he must have been spending his time in the greenhouse as usual.

The greenhouse was one of Elsie's grievances. What smart house had a greenhouse leaning up against it nowadays, she was for ever asking Joe. It ought to have been pulled down long ago to make way for a garage. But Joe, so docile in most ways, stuck firmly to his greenhouse and said there was no need for a garage without a car to put in it. Elsie said there ought to be a car and said it very often. She also said that even if there was no car, a house looked better with a garage; it gave a better impression.

Besides, what was the good of a greenhouse, she wanted to know, if Joe didn't grow something useful in it? Something that could be turned to account. Why should she have to spend money on potted ferns and aspidistras for the house when he could have grown them in the greenhouse? Goodness only knew she didn't want to spend money on pot-plants; she needed all the money she could get for other things. There were dozens of things she ought to have. The house Joe had brought her to was a disgrace. So old-fashioned. His first wife could have had no taste at all. The furniture was all old mahogany stuff and everybody knew mahogany had quite gone out. There wasn't a suite in the place; simply nothing that matched anything else at all. As fast as she could, Elsie was getting rid of the old things and replacing them with suites. She had a beauty in the bedroom now; limed oak with turquoise-blue bakelite handles. This replacement cost money and she did think Joe might help by growing pot-plants in the greenhouse.

But the greenhouse was almost entirely taken up by a climbing rose, one of those old-fashioned dark red roses that smelled all right, but were no use whatever in vases. The rose-tree was now in full bloom, but Elsie would not have any of the roses in the house. In addition to the fact that they would not stand up in her silver vases, she had a grudge against the tree. Joe spent far too much time with it; he was for ever doing something to it, tying up, watering, syringing, cutting off dead heads when he might have been taking her to a show or going round with her to call on the Watsons. She wasn't going to encourage him by admitting the roses to the house or admiring the tree in any way. Besides, she didn't admire it.

'If it had been an American Beauty now,' she said to him.

It would have been all right if he had brought sheaves of those long-stemmed buds to her like the young men on the films.

Joe spent most of his spare time in the greenhouse and the garden but she could never see much result from it. They said his first wife was fond of gardening. Perhaps that's what had brought them together, she thought. It couldn't be much else; she looked a poor plain thing from her photograph.

'You couldn't say that about me,' thought Elsie, pinching up her permanent waves.

She was pretty and young and smart, and she wanted a smart house and a smart husband. The house she would get, in time, but the husband she often despaired of. There he was going out of the gate now, stooping as badly as ever, after all she'd told him. She rapped on the window and when Joe looked round, she stood smartly to attention. Joe understood, obediently straightened his shoulders and went on out of the gate and down the long road, almost empty at this hour of the summer morning.

'At any rate, I've done something towards improving his appearance,' thought Elsie.

Before she married him he had gone about in a bowler hat, brown kid gloves and the kind of overcoat affected by undertakers. Now she had taken his overcoat away and given him yellow gloves and a black felt hat. He certainly looked better, but the hat seemed to be resting now on the tops of his ears, she noted with dissatisfaction. Strange that nothing looked right long on Joe.

There was Mrs Watson now, coming up the road towards him. In a new coat and skirt. New; though she hadn't been wearing her other any time at all. Elsie was upset by Mrs Watson's new coat and skirt. It made her feel she'd have to have a new coat and skirt too, though she had meant to wear the one she'd got until the end of the season. But if *Mrs Watson* was going to flaunt a new coat and skirt . . .

Mrs Watson and Joe were drawing level. Now surely Joe was going to raise his hat properly after all her instructions? She had told him many a time that he mustn't merely touch the crown of his hat, but must lift his hat right off his head, lift it high and bow in the gentlemanly, slightly foreign way Elsie admired so much in young Mr Heatherington. Yes, Joe had remembered. He was lifting his hat high from his head. But what was that? What had fallen from it? Something red. A red rose. A red rose lay on the pavement between Joe and Mrs Watson. And now Joe was bending to pick up the rose. He was putting it back into his hat, putting his hat on his head and now he had hurried round the corner out of sight. Mrs Watson was standing to look after him and Elsie looked too. She stood at the window, looking in stupefaction.

Joe with a rose in his hat! Joe, so mild, middle-aged, bald and stooping, with a rose in his hat for a woman. Oh, most certainly a woman. Now she knew why he spent his time in the greenhouse. Now it flashed upon her. All that time, all that care so that he could take a rose in his hat to a woman.

'After all I've done,' cried Elsie. ' Me! At my age and with my looks I took him on when no one else like me would have looked at him. I take him on and spend all my energy smartening him up and bringing him into line and instead of going down on his bended knees in gratitude, he's taking a rose every day to another woman.'

Who was it? Wildly she cast about in her mind and brought up the answer. That Miss Bond. That girl at his office. A minx if ever there was one. Miss Bond was another of the things Elsie had determined to clear out, but she had been so busy she hadn't got to her yet and now it was too late. Joe was taking her roses. The shameful fickleness of men made Elsie burn with indignation. Joe was nothing much in the way of a man, but he'd married one woman and when she died, he'd married a second and now he was off after a third.

'But I'll show you,' said Elsie through her teeth. 'You've reckoned without me, Joe Smith.'

She rushed into her bedroom and snatching open the new wardrobe, brought out her hat and coat. She kicked off her slippers and thrust her feet into her outdoor shoes. Panting with haste, tears and agitation, she ran down the stairs, out of the front door, down the garden path, down the long road. She had been quick and Joe was not yet out of sight. Holding her coat together, her eyes intent on his back, her lips folded, she followed him. Creeping under the walls, slackening her speed when he slackened his, dodging into doorways when she thought he was going to look back, letting him turn corners, then running noiselessly to keep up with him, she went after him through the little town. As far as she was concerned there might have been nobody in it but her and Joe and Miss Bond at the office.

Joe's office was at the far side of an old square in the centre of the town. The parish church stood in the square and the shortest way to the office was across the churchyard. Hunching his shoulders, Joe turned into the churchyard and Elsie came behind him as stealthily as a thief in the night. The office was near now, the moment was near.

'I'll wait in the church porch,' she said to herself. 'I'll give him time to get in and then I'll catch them at it.'

She dodged into the porch and stood there, her breast heaving. But she could not wait long; she was too eager to precipitate the moment of discovery. When she came out of the porch, Joe was only just going out at the other side of the churchyard.

'Why doesn't he get on?' she fumed. 'He's slow – slow as ever even with a rose in his hat!'

She waited, trembling with impatience, bursting with all she was going to say; then, as he passed out of sight, she ran down the path.

But what was that? That splash of red to the left? Elsie halted and then came slowly up. The rose lay at the foot of a white marble cross inscribed: 'In loving memory of Alice, wife of Joseph . . .'

All the heat went out of Elsie standing on the path. In the sun the grave of Alice flashed triumphant, indestructible, with the rose laid upon it. Joe was not fickle; he was only too faithful.

'I'd rather it had been the typist,' thought poor Elsie turning away. 'You can't fight – that.'

YOUTH

Miss Morley and her young niece were spending a day in town for a treat. For strange as it might seem to anyone outside these islands, a day in London, in spite of possible raids, was still a treat. London was London still; in fact it was more than ever wonderful, and at the mere mention of its name, every heart stirred with love and admiration.

Miss Morley was a busy woman. Even in the desert, surrounded by nothing but sand and scrub, Miss Morley would have been able to be busy. The village, though small, was far from being a desert, and Miss Morley found it a full-time occupation. Just as Miss Morley's little eighteenth-century house on the green dominated the village, so Miss Morley dominated village affairs, running the Mothers' Union, the Women's Institute, the school, and as far as possible, the church, without much opposition. In discussions and at meetings, when Miss Morley began, other people generally gave up. They had not the energy she had. Their store of energy had been depleted by other things: lack of money, large families, ill-health or something from which Miss Morley seemed to be immune. The circumstances of her life had set Miss Morley at liberty to get her own way, and she mostly got it.

The arrival of evacuees in the village had given Miss Morley further chances to be busy with their feeding, entertainment and general supervision, but it was more difficult to deal with evacuees than with the villagers, who had been under her thumb for years, and Miss Morley had noticed of late that she was losing her temper rather frequently. She had usually been losing her temper for a long time before she noticed it herself, but when finally she did notice it, she came to the conclusion that she must be tired and in need of a little change. This time she decided to knock off for a day and take Anne up to London. Anne, aged eighteen, was enraptured, and here they were on a fine June morning, sitting opposite each other in the crowded train.

They did not talk much, separated as they were, but Anne kept sending flying glances of excitement at her aunt. She kept smiling, though she remembered not to, now and again, in case other passengers thought her odd, smiling to herself so incessantly.

Anne was radiant in a suit of spring green, with a green cap set far back on her shining hair. Miss Morley looked with satisfaction at Anne's hair, pale gold, swinging to her shoulders and most becomingly turned under at the ends. A simple and lovely style, thought Miss Morley, and she was responsible for it. She had allowed and supervised Anne's first permanent wave.

'Only three minutes, please,' said Miss Morley sternly to the hairdresser. 'The thing must not be overdone.'

It was not. The result was enchanting. It was so successful that Miss Morley actually had her own hair permanently waved. She grew the ends of the shingle she had worn for fifteen years and had them arranged in close-lying curls. It made a great difference to her appearance, and Miss Morley spent much more time admiring her back hair with the aid of a hand-mirror than anyone in the village would have believed. In fact, if Miss Morley had had her hair waved years ago, she might have been a different woman altogether.

Miss Morley congratulated herself on Anne's hair and also on Anne's green suit. She had chosen it. Anne had an allowance from her father, but Miss Morley managed it for her. Miss Morley had managed everything for Anne, Anne included, since Anne had been sent home from India as a child. Her mother was dead, her father a soldier in the Indian Army, not due to retire for many years yet. It looked as if nothing would remove Anne from her aunt's management but marriage, and Miss Morley did not encourage marriage in those about her.

Miss Morley considered that she herself had missed nothing in missing marriage. She had, materially, everything she wanted, and through Anne she had enjoyed all the pleasures of motherhood without its troubles. Not that there ought to be any troubles, said Miss Morley, entitled, through Anne, to pronounce on this subject. When mothers confided to her that they had difficulty with their daughters, Miss Morley breezily remarked that she simply couldn't understand it. She had none with Anne.

'Nearly there,' said Anne now, with another of her fleeting smiles.

Anne had wanted to be a dancer, but Miss Morley would not hear of it. She had chosen a career in Domestic Science for her instead. But owing to the stupidity, according to Miss Morley, of those she termed the education authorities, Anne was spending a year at home. Her school had requested her to leave, since she had passed School Certificate and there was no room, in the evacuation premises, for those whose school career was finished. Anne left school, but could not go to college until after her eighteenth birthday. It turned out that she had been most inconveniently born. Her eighteenth birthday fell in November, after the college year had started. She could not enter until the following year, when she would be almost nineteen. It was all very stupid, her aunt considered, but she was secretly enjoying Anne's company.

It was pleasant to see a young face across the table, to hear a young voice calling about the garden and the house.

'I'm just looking out at the trees. Aren't they beautiful? I think this is the dearest house in the world, Aunt Bea.'

'Well, it shall be yours some day.' Miss Morley would say to herself.

It was nice to think Anne would have her things, nice that there was someone to have them. If it had not been for Anne, all she had accumulated through the years would have gone to sales and to strangers.

Miss Morley had accumulated a good many things, because, though so occupied and so fortunate in her house, her good maids, her charming garden, she sometimes felt that life was flat and empty. When she felt like that, she bought herself something, a piece of Georgian silver, or antique glass, or embroidery. These things consoled and interested her for a time and she felt better. But after a while, they ceased to interest her and she had to buy something else. But during Anne's year at home, she hadn't had to buy anything.

'We're there,' Anne cried.

She sprang up, the train stopped, the doors flew open. Out poured the passengers, a very large proportion of them men in uniform, airmen, soldiers, sailors.

'Oh, Aunt Bea, aren't they wonderful?' cried Anne, turning round incessantly as they made their way up the platform.

'Don't keep turning round, dear. It looks very bad,' said Miss Morley pleasantly.

'Nobody's looking at me,' said Anne, 'and I do want to look at them. We never see any of these wonderful men in the village. Isn't the RAF uniform perfectly fascinating?'

'Look where you are going, dear,' said her aunt. 'We mustn't get separated.'

Anne took Miss Morley's arm to prevent this.

'Oh, it's all so exciting,' she breathed, as they went through the barrier. 'I love the village, but, oh, it is wonderful to come *out*, Aunt Bea, isn't it.'

'There's our bus,' said Miss Morley.

The morning was to be Miss Morley's; most of it would be spent in the shops. But the afternoon was Anne's to do as she liked with, her aunt conceded, only to wish at once that she hadn't. She expected Anne to say: 'Let's go to a theatre,' which was what she herself wanted to do. Instead, Anne said: 'Oh, thank you, Aunt Bea! I choose, *of course*, to go to the Thé-Dansant at the Hotel Imperial.'

Miss Morley had forgotten about dancing. Dancing, at her age, meant nothing at all. It gave her a shock when Anne spoke of a Thé-Dansant, reminding her of a world where such things still went on. She had grown middle-aged, she was entirely occupied with what she thought of as 'good works', but youth was still dancing. The world was at war, but youth was still dancing. This was a strange thought for Miss Morley and she wanted neither to go to a Dance-Tea at the Hotel Imperial herself nor to take Anne there. But since she prided herself on being a woman who kept her word, she had to go.

'I don't know why you want to go,' she could not help saying, 'you won't be able to dance. *I* shan't dance with you, you know.'

'Oh, of course not,' cried Anne, looking, her aunt thought, unnecessarily horrified, 'but I want to watch the dancing and I do want to hear that band. It's a very special band, you know.'

'Now, how do you know that?' asked Miss Morley, inclined to carp.

'Because I hear it on the wireless.'

Miss Morley was silent. Dance bands were never heard when she was in the house. She saw to that. Anne must turn them on when she was out. Miss Morley felt there was something rather rebellious and deceitful about that and compressed her lips.

They arrived at the entrance of the famous Hotel Imperial and Miss Morley hung back. Behind her was the bright day, before her the gloom of the vast hall, lit, even at this early hour of the afternoon, by rosy-shaded lamps.

'Waste of a fine day to go in there,' said Miss Morley.

But Anne, already half-way across the hall, turned, like

Proserpina entering the underworld, to beckon on an elderly tweed-clad relative, and Miss Morley reluctantly followed. Anne pressed on to the ballroom and, like a child come to a party, her eager eyes ran over the lights and the flowers, the shining floor diminished to a more intimate square by carpets and small tables set for tea.

'Isn't it lovely?' she said, with a happy sigh.

'There's nobody here,' said Miss Morley. 'But I'm not surprised. People have more sense.'

'Let's get a table next to the floor,' said Anne, eagerly making her way there. 'See, this table's reserved, and that's reserved and that and that,' she pointed. 'Lots of people are coming, Aunt Bea. It's a good thing we got here early. Shall we have this one?'

'It's all the same to me,' said Miss Morley, laying down her parcels and umbrella with resignation.

Anne, her eyes wide with excitement, sat opposite and drew off her gloves. The orchestra was tuning up; it twittered like birds waking in the morning. The flute-player played a little tune of his own for the sheer love of it.

'Isn't this part exciting?' said Anne. 'Like before the curtain goes up in the theatre. I think the last few moments before things start are terribly exciting.'

The orchestra began to play a Strauss waltz.

'Oh, that heavenly waltz and that lovely empty floor,' said Anne, clasping her hands. 'I suppose I couldn't just go out and dance by myself while there's no one here?'

'Of course not,' said Miss Morley, 'it would look too absurd. Besides, people are coming in now.'

People were flocking in, refuting Miss Morley's belief in their sanity. The tables filled up. It was an assembly of youth; airmen, soldiers, young naval officers with girls and young women. Here and there a table was occupied by older women come to have tea and to look on. But the dancers, who swept out on to the floor at once, as if they were afraid of wasting a moment, were all young.

Anne watched them. Excitement died out of her eyes and her face grew wistful. Watching these others, she longed, she longed to dance. There was some awful void in life. There was something, someone, calling with the music. No, it was herself calling, and there was no one to answer.

She turned her head away so that Aunt Bea, who would never understand, should not see the longing in her face. Her heart swelled. Oh, to dance, to dance. Not only to dance, but to be with a companion of her youth, of her heart. She felt excluded, shut out from life. These others were happy, they were together, and only she was left out, left to sit and look on, to take no part.

A girl in the orchestra began to sing:

'You get a kick from stormy weather, And so do I. And so do I.'

To be able to say that, thought Anne, to feel that with someone.

'Of all the rubbish!' exclaimed Miss Morley. 'That's not music. It's moaning. That girl isn't singing, she's just saying those ridiculous words in a very hoarse speaking voice. A kick from stormy weather, indeed; I've hardly the patience to sit here.'

'I love that song,' said Anne dreamily, unaware that her aunt had spoken.

Her wistful eyes, wandering, fell on a table, where a young airman sat alone. Her interest quickened and she forgot the dancing. This was one of the heroes. This young man with curly hair had done splendid daring things. Glowing with admiration, Anne observed him. He smoked. He drank tea. He watched the dancers. Something in his attitude, his elbow on the table, his long legs extended to the very edge of the floor, told her he wasn't waiting for anyone. He was not only alone, he was lonely.

The young man, coming to the end of his cigarette and feeling in his case for another, turned his head and met her eyes across the wide corner that separated their tables. Anne looked hastily away; she mustn't seem to stare. But his eyes remained on her.

In a moment, she stole another glance. He was still looking at her. She blushed, one of the quick, lovely blushes of youth, and tried to pay attention to what Aunt Bea was saying.

'We'd have been far better at the theatre,' said Miss Morley. 'I think even you will agree that this is all very dull.'

Dull?

Anne's heart beat fast. She felt his eyes on her and she didn't know where to look to avoid them. Her own eyes made a naïve circuit all round him.

The music stopped and the dancers trooped back to their tables. Waiters brought fresh tea, and in the bustle Anne looked at him again. He was looking deeply at her as if he had never looked away.

Anne made a determined effort. She crossed her long slender legs, clasped her knee and, leaning well forward, looked carefully in the opposite direction. But a burning awareness had been set up between her and the young man, and in a moment, intuition made her turn suddenly towards him.

He was pressing out the stub of his cigarette. He was getting up. He pulled down his tunic and put a nervous hand to his tie. Skirting the dance floor, making his way between the tables, all eyes rising to him as he passed, he was coming to her. Anne, her cheeks flushed, eyes wide, lips parted, watched him come. She swallowed visibly and Miss Morley, her glance falling on her niece with amazement, whipped round to see what she could be looking at. The young man had just reached their table.

'Will you allow me to introduce myself?' he said.

'Pilot-Officer Geoffrey Lawton. May I have the pleasure of the next dance?' he said to Anne.

Anne gazed at him, transfixed by shyness, dumb.

Miss Morley took swift charge of the situation.

'My niece is not dancing, thank you,' she said, her head turned upwards over her raised shoulder, like a hen protecting its nest from an eagle.

The young man flushed, as if she had struck him in the face. Then he bowed.

'I beg your pardon,' he said grimly, turning away.

Cups poised, scones half-way to mouths, everybody had watched the young airman approach the very pretty girl in green. Everybody had seen him rebuffed by the elderly chaperone, and now everybody watched him make his way back among the tables again. Then all, it seemed by common consent, turned to look at Anne and Miss Morley.

Anne had gone very red, then very white. Miss Morley sat up stiff and straight. Suddenly both, finding their voices, leaned across the table, Miss Morley talking Anne down with determination.

'Did you encourage that young man to come across to this table?' she demanded.

'No, I didn't. I didn't know he was going to come. I've been looking at him, though, and he's been looking at me. But what harm is there in that? Airmen are worth looking at. I want to look at them . . .'

The young man had reached his table. He sat down. He was young enough to take papers from his pocket and pretend to examine them to give himself countenance. His face assumed a look of hard indifference that cut Anne to the quick.

'There's no need to get so heated, Anne,' Miss Morley was saying with severity. 'I shall take good care you don't come to this sort of place again, since this is what you subject me to.'

'Why shouldn't he ask me to dance? Why?' persisted Anne, who seemed, to her scandalised aunt, to be on the verge of bursting into tears. Here, in a public place where everyone was taking far too much interest in the scene.

'You know nothing whatever about him . . .'

'I know he risks his life for us. Surely I can risk a *dance* for him,' said Anne.

'Anne.'

But Anne would not be silenced.

'I hated it for him when he had to go back when you said no and everybody knew,' she burst out incoherently. 'It was awful for him. He minded. He minded very badly. I saw. When he was walking away, his neck was all red at the back. Those other soldiers all knew you'd refused. They laughed. They were sorry for him, but they laughed. Besides, Aunt Bea,' said Anne, with sudden adult dignity, 'you should have allowed me to answer for myself. It was me he asked to dance.'

'Silence, Anne,' said Miss Morley with suppressed violence. 'You're behaving abominably.'

'I think it was you who behaved abominably,' said Anne steadily. 'You should never have treated him like that.'

Miss Morley gasped.

The orchestra was playing again. It was playing:

You are the promised kiss of springtime
That makes the lonely winter seem so long.

Anne rose from her chair. Miss Morley's horror-stricken eyes rose with her.

'Anne, sit down,' she said.

But Anne continued to stand. Slender, shy, she stood gathering her courage. Then she moved quickly between the tables, skirted the edge of the dance-floor, which, because of the interest everyone was taking in her, was still empty, and reached the table of the young airman, who did not look up from his papers or know she was there till she spoke.

Standing beside him, she said in a voice that shook a little: 'Will you dance with me, please?'

He looked up. Relief and pleasure cleared his face. He stood up, thrusting his papers into his pocket. He looked as if he couldn't believe his luck. He held out one hand and she laid hers in it. His other arm encircled her, and in the beauty of their youth, they swung out into the dance. As they passed Miss Morley, now entirely forgotten by both of them, they smiled into each other's eyes.

THE HANDBAG

Mrs West had been alone for the weekend, but there was nothing new in that. William was often away. He didn't tell her where he was going and she would not ask. He merely said he wouldn't be at home on Tuesday, or Wednesday, or at the weekend, or whenever it was.

But Mrs West generally managed to find out where he had gone by going through the papers in his desk. He meant to keep the desk locked, but he often forgot and his wife took every advantage of that.

William had plenty of opportunity of getting away. He was a Councillor; probably he would shortly be an Alderman, the youngest Alderman, and probably, too, the Leader of his Party. He was very anxious to secure these honours and his wife knew he was being careful to keep in with everybody.

As a Councillor and a member of the Health, Education, Gas and other committees, William attended many Conferences. His wife used to go with him and she enjoyed them very much. They were always held at such pleasant places, at Brighton, Harrogate, Bournemouth for instance, and they stayed at the best hotels. The Corporation paid William's first-class expenses and he used to manage to make those do for both of them.

That was all over now. William first took to making excuses for not taking her, then he went without her without making excuses, and now he did not even tell her when or where he was going. The higher William rose in public life, the further he pushed her into the background.

She had discovered lately that he was making her out to be an invalid. People stopped her in the street to ask with sympathy how she was.

'Such a pity you weren't well enough to come to the Ball the other night,' someone would say, and Mrs West was obliged to smile and accept her imaginary illness because she would not let it be known that William had never told her about the Ball.

Dinners, luncheons, receptions, prize-distributions, William went to them all without her. She knew nothing of them until she saw an account of them in the paper, with Councillor William West prominently mentioned, or until such time as she found the desk unlocked and went through the discarded invitations. All of them were inscribed for Councillor and Mrs West, yet he never told her of them and she was too proud to charge him with them.

She didn't know precisely why he behaved in this way. She thought there must be several reasons. William had always been a vain man, but the older he got the vainer he became. He was forty-eight – she was the same age, but looked older – he was handsome in a dark, increasingly florid way and he fancied himself considerably on a platform. He liked to show off, but not before his wife. He felt she judged him. She cramped his style, she knew when he was not telling the truth. He felt freer without her.

Mrs West also surmised that William was ashamed of her. She was plain, she had no taste in dress. She had done her own housework and economised for years, though they had maids and were prosperous now. There were no frills about her, she admitted, but she had made William very comfortable and had borne with his exacting, uncertain, often foolish behaviour for more than twenty years. She surmised, shrewdly, that William valued his comfortable home, his good food, but no longer wished to be seen about with the one who secured these things for him. He was ashamed of her. She wasn't smart enough for him.

If she had been Mrs Wintersley, now, it would have been different, thought Mrs West, sitting alone over the week-end. Mrs Wintersley was a youngish widow who had lately entered public affairs and taken her place on the Council. Mrs Wintersley was smart, there was no doubt about that. She had made quite a commotion on the Council and was in enormous demand at public functions: Prize Distributions, Women's Luncheon Clubs, the openings of schools, bazaars and so on.

Mrs West had seen Mrs Wintersley many a time, though Mrs Wintersley did not know who she was. Mrs Wintersley would probably have been astonished, thought Mrs West, to discover that the plain little woman sitting at the next table at the Rosebowl Tea Rooms the other day was the wife of the resplendent William West.

Mrs Wintersley had heard Mrs West's voice, because Mrs West often answered the telephone when Mrs Wintersley rang William up. Mrs Wintersley was always ringing William up. Mrs West supposed it was all right; they were both on the Council.

At the Rosebowl Tea Rooms, Mrs West had enjoyed her obscurity and had taken the opportunity of observing Mrs Wintersley very closely. She didn't like her, she decided. She was very well dressed and very well made-up, but she had a hard mouth and restless eyes, eyes always seeking for an audience. A person, Mrs West concluded, who could not live without limelight. She was afraid William was also like that.

Mrs Wintersley, when Mrs West had seen her before, had generally been in black, but on this particular afternoon she wore becoming blue-green tweeds. Everything about her toilet was carefully chosen as usual and Mrs West noticed that even her handbag exactly matched her suit. It was made of the same blue-green tweed and as it lay on the table while Mrs Wintersley had tea, Mrs West observed it, as she observed everything else about Mrs Wintersley.

Going through William's desk in his absence over the weekend, Mrs West had come upon an invitation for Tuesday evening to the Speech Day at the Girls' Grammar School. The Address and the Prizes, the paste-board announced, would be given by Councillor Mrs Wintersley and the invitation was inscribed as usual: 'Councillor and Mrs West. Platform.'

At the beginning of William's public career, Mrs West had often been asked to give prizes and she had managed, she thought, rather well. At any rate, William used to congratulate her in those days, when they were both new to the platform together. But of course, Mrs West thought diffidently, William had left her far behind long ago.

The invitation was for Tuesday and it was Tuesday now. On the previous day William had returned from wherever it was he had been; Mrs West had not been able to find out where this was, since there was no reference to any conference in his desk.

William was now seated at the breakfast table, buried behind the paper. Mrs West had finished breakfast and was just about to leave the table when the maid brought in the morning post. William lowered the paper long enough to see that there was nothing for him before disappearing behind it again. For Mrs West, however, there was a parcel. She wondered what it could be. She rarely received parcels unless she sent for something from the London shops. Holding the parcel on her knee, out of the way of the breakfast things, she undid the wrappings.

Within them lay, of all unexpected things, a green tweed bag.

Mrs West stared uncomprehendingly. A green tweed bag?

Then, glancing towards William and observing that he was still buried behind the paper and had seen nothing, Mrs West bundled the bag back into its wrappings and took it swiftly out of the room. She hurried upstairs, stumbling in her haste, and gained her bedroom. Locking the door, she tumbled the bag from its wrappings again. There was a letter with it. With shaking fingers she drew the sheet of notepaper from the envelope. It was headed: The Troutfishers Inn, Patondale, and was addressed to Mrs West, 3 The Mount, Lynchester.

Dear Madam,

We have pleasure in returning to you a handbag found
in room number sixteen after you had left this
morning. . . .

Mrs West went slowly to her bed and sat down upon it.
The bag was Mrs Wintersley's. She would have known it any-
where. But why had it been sent to her? Why addressed to
Mrs West, at 3 The Mount?

It took Mrs West several minutes to grasp the truth. William
and Mrs Wintersley had spent the weekend at the Troutfishers'
Inn together. A flush of anger, humiliation and hurt rose in
Mrs West's faded cheek. She knew William was foolish, vain,
unkind, but she had never thought, she told herself, that he
would do this kind of thing. Never.

She sat on the bed, her head low.

What a fool he was! He was endangering the very thing
he cared most about – his public career. Aldermen were not
allowed moral lapses; at least they must never be found out.
But William, fool that he was, had registered at the inn in his
own name. He had done that, she knew, because of his fixed
idea that everybody knew him everywhere. He would think it
useless to attempt to hide his importance under an assumed
name. But he would suppose, and rightly, that no one knew
his wife. No one did know her. He had seen to that. It would
therefore be quite safe, he would think, for Mrs Wintersley
to pose as Mrs West. But she had left this bag behind – there
was nothing in it but a handkerchief and a lipstick with no

incriminating mark of ownership on either – and they had sent it to the address William had given in the book.

Mrs West sat on the bed, the bag beside her, turning things over in her mind.

'William,' she said at lunch. 'I think I shall go to the Speech Day at the Girls' Grammar School tonight.'

William looked up.

'I haven't accepted for you,' he said.

'That's all right,' said Mrs West equably. 'I rang up the Headmistress this morning to say I should be there.'

William frowned.

'Why should you go?' he said. 'It will be very boring.'

'All the same,' she said calmly. 'I think I shall go.'

And at eight o'clock she was there, in a moleskin coat and a straw hat with a blue rose in it, waiting in an ante-room with the rest of the 'platform' for the arrival of Mrs Wintersley. William looked put out. Mrs West knew it was because she was there, but she didn't mind. She felt quite easy and comfortable; it was someone else's turn to be humiliated now, she told herself.

Mrs Wintersley arrived, beautifully dressed in black with a tiny hat, a floating veil and a bunch of lilies of the valley pinned under her chin. She was effusively greeted by everybody, including William. Mrs West stood apart, but when the Headmistress, in her Oxford hood, reading out the names of the guests and their places on the platform came to the name of Mrs West, that lady saw Mrs Wintersley turn sharply in astonishment. Mrs West felt her prolonged stare of amused surprise, but she herself continued to smile imperturbably from under her straw hat. Let Mrs Wintersley smile while she could, she thought.

Mrs West found that she had been given a place of honour next to Mrs Wintersley, with William beside her. Nothing could have been more convenient to her purpose.

'Shall we go?' said the Headmistress.

As they filed out, Mrs Wintersley fell back to speak to William West.

'I left my bag behind at the inn,' she said in an undertone.

'Good Lord,' he exclaimed. 'How did that happen? I thought women never moved without their bags.'

'It wasn't the one I ordinarily use. It was the one that matches my tweed suit. There was nothing in it.'

'That's better,' said William. 'Well, I'll write and ask them to return it to the office.'

Mrs Wintersley's face cleared. She advanced, amidst a burst of handclapping, to her place on the platform.

Mrs West followed her. It was quite pleasant, she thought, to be at one of these affairs again. She liked the rows of young faces below her, the palms beside her, the flowers, the long table covered with a ceremonial cloth and piled with suitable literature, silver cups, shields and medals.

Behind the front row of the platform there were other rows containing people of less importance, minor councillors, mistresses, and so on.

The Press took flashlight photographs of Mrs Wintersley with Mrs West small beside her and William towering beyond. The platform then sat down and the school sang its opening song.

The Headmistress came behind William and asked him, in the absence of the Mayor, to propose the vote of thanks to Mrs Wintersley later. William nodded importantly, exchanged a glance with Mrs Wintersley and began to make notes on a small card concealed in the palm of his hand.

After the song, the Headmistress announced that she would read her report.

While she read, Mrs Wintersley sat gracefully, conning her notes or smiling at the girls. Mrs West rather grimly regarded her. She did not hear a word of the report. It was over before she realised it and she had to hasten to join in the applause.

There was another song. Mrs Wintersley received a few whispered instructions from the Headmistress. The address, Mrs West had long ago noted on her programme, was to be given next, before the distribution of the prizes.

The song ended; the school sat down again. The Headmistress rose to announce that she had the greatest pleasure in asking Mrs Wintersley to give her address. A few words in eulogy of Mrs Wintersley and the admirable work she was doing in the city followed and amid great applause Mrs Wintersley rose.

She stood there, waiting for the clapping to die down and Mrs West looking up at her, saw the confident smile and the sparkle in her eyes. Mrs Wintersley was collecting her audience; she was enjoying herself.

At a sign from the Headmistress, the applause ceased. There was silence, a hush of expectancy. Mrs Wintersley, with a slight cough, laid one finely-gloved hand on the table and in her ringing voice began:

'Ladies and gentlemen. Girls.'

She inhaled a long breath.

'I am very glad . . .' she said.

As if she were tired of holding it, Mrs West brought from under her voluminous moleskin sleeve a wholly unsuitable green tweed bag and laid it on the table beside the prizes.

'I am very honoured,' Mrs Wintersley was saying, 'to have been asked to come here tonight . . .'

Distracted by the movement on the table under her eyes, Mrs Wintersley, frowning in annoyance, glanced down. She came to a dead stop. Her voice dying on the listening air, Mrs Wintersley stared in as much horror at the green tweed bag as Macbeth at the apparition of the dagger.

With an audible gasp, she put out a shaking hand towards it. The platform, the school craned in amazement to see what it was that had so affected her. The Headmistress stood with a petrified stare. William West half-rose to his feet, watching the approach of Mrs Wintersley's hand towards the green tweed bag. But on the very point of touching it, Mrs Wintersley suddenly snatched back her hand as if something had burnt it. With a hoarse exclamation, she turned on Mrs West. But the sight of that lady smiling imperturbably from under her straw hat seemed to complete Mrs Wintersley's strange collapse. She whipped round, turning her back on the school, presenting a convulsed face to the platform.

'I . . . I . . .' she stammered. 'I can't go on . . . Something . . . I'm not well. I'm . . . Let me pass, please.'

Plunging through the chairs, the occupants of which got hurriedly up to make way for her, tripping clumsily over the

red drugget laid down in her honour, Mrs Wintersley rushed
headlong from the platform. In the staring silence, her smart
hat awry, her veil flying, her high heels rattling loudly over
the wooden floor, Mrs Wintersley fled down the length of the
hall, followed, to the astonishment of all, by Councillor William
West.

As they made their amazing exit through the door at the
end of the hall, uproar broke out. Five hundred girls, their
parents and the occupants of the platform burst into excited
comment. The Headmistress, stern, drawn to her full height,
struck on her bell. But silence did not follow. Confusion continued to reign. The Headmistress advanced to the front of
the platform and with lips compressed struck the bell again
and again and again. She struck until the tongues were still
and all eyes upon her. Then calmly and coldly she spoke:

'Mrs Wintersley is evidently indisposed,' she said. 'But she
will be adequately taken care of and our programme must
go on. There will be no address. We shall proceed at once to the
distribution of the prizes. Er . . .' The Headmistress faltered
in her turn. She looked uncertainly behind and around her.
Who could give the prizes now? Who was there important
enough? She stood there, at a loss. Mrs West leaned forward
from her place, smiling helpfully. 'Shall *I* give the prizes?' she
said.

FAMILY CRISIS

I

The shop was empty, but that did not trouble Mr Parker, who had done good business as usual all day. It was natural and convenient that the shop should be empty towards closing time and Mr Parker stood behind the counter, waiting to shut it up and go home.

Mr Parker was a highly respectable man. He prided himself upon respecting and being respected, and as he stood in his shop on this Monday evening in August, he looked as he wished to look, extremely respectable. He was small, thin, middle-aged and very neat in his dress; a refined type, he often thought. He wore a suit of summer grey, a wing collar and a bow-tie, which he always tried to keep straight, but which, in spite of him, was often crooked.

His very expression was respectable, slightly pinched and disapproving, as he stood with his hand on an order he had made out for Cave, Scorseby's traveller, who was due today, but who was either going to come very late or not going to come at all.

Mr Parker was a chemist and nothing could have suited him

better. It was such clean work and the neat little packets of powders that Mr Parker made up, the neat little boxes of pills, the bottles of medicine wrapped in white paper, sealed with red wax and disposed in rows like spotless miniature mummies were very satisfying to Mr Parker's orderly soul.

Besides, in no other capacity but as a chemist could Mr Parker have been brought into such intimate contact with the best people in the town. He often came near to thanking God that he was not as other men are, as other tradesmen, that is, for if he had been an ironmonger, for instance, a grocer or a draper, he would not have been consulted so confidentially by Mrs Burton of Sefton Lodge about her elastic stocking, by Major Morton about his truss, by old Lady Worthing about how to keep her false teeth in, or by Miss Steadman on some new way of counteracting the effects of constant overeating. The ailments and weaknesses of the best people in the town were an open book to Mr Parker in his capacity as chemist and this was of peculiar satisfaction to him. The people before mentioned, together with the Randalls, the Handleys, the Gores and Miss Fanny Martin were all his good customers; Mr Parker's definition of a good customer being a person of the upper classes who spent a lot on medicine.

Mr Parker's admiration for the upper classes, although it had begun as a harmless idealism was degenerating into snobbery and becoming a nuisance to all about him. Mr Parker was, however, on the point of being pulled up. Life always seems to hit a man in his most sensitive part.

It had been hot in the town all day, with baking white pavements and the tar soft in the gutters, but the shop was cool. The temperature in Mr Parker's shop was always right; in winter pleasantly warm, in summer cool and the smell always the same, a combination of toilet soap, antiseptics and cough lozenges. The shop itself was spacious and dignified, with mahogany fittings and drawers and bottles lettered in Latin and gilt. Mr Parker prided himself on the fact that he had got his shop very well arranged; everything in order and everything of the best quality.

He had got his life well-arranged too. He was doing well himself and his son Alec was doing even better. He was very proud of Alec, who was now the junior partner of a firm of solicitors in Liverpool. Alec had absorbed and carried further his father's precepts on self-improvement. 'Always play with someone a bit better than yourself,' had been one of them. Mr Parker had come across it in a book and it seemed such excellent advice for children that he had passed it on to his. The seed fell on receptive ground in Alec and on stony in Margaret. At any rate Margaret had seemed not to profit from it in the way of making nice friends, or indeed any friends at all.

Mr Parker had made and demanded many sacrifices for Alec. Just as he had a fixed idea about the upper classes, looking at them through rose-coloured spectacles, unable to perceive that they were as good and as bad, as different among themselves as any other class, so also Mr Parker had a fixed idea about sons. A son was every man's dream and hope, and he did not see Alec as he was, but as a son.

It had cost a good deal to article Alec, maintain him in Liverpool – Alec had decided he would succeed better in

Liverpool than in his native town where everybody would always know, he said, that his father kept a shop – and it cost more to buy him the junior partnership. The Parker family had to economize and one of the ways that suggested itself to Mr Parker was that they should do without a maid at home. Margaret was just leaving school and Mr Parker said she could help her mother in the house. They must manage between them, he said. They did manage, but not between them. It was Margaret who managed.

She was seventeen when she started managing and was now twenty-three. She did not complain, but she resented the fact that, after managing all week, she could not relax at the weekend because Alec came home from his rooms in Liverpool then. A great fuss, devolving upon Margaret, was made for him, not only because his father liked to give Alec the best of everything, but because Alec was caustic if he didn't get it. He was a very critical young man and if things were not exactly as he thought they ought to be, he said so, in a cold way implying that his family really ought to know better and that if they mixed with the people he mixed with, they probably would. This, instead of wounding, served only to increase the admiration his father felt for him.

Mr Parker, standing at the counter, glanced at his watch. Cave wasn't going to turn up today. He was due and he hadn't come. Mr Parker was annoyed. He liked things to be done at their appointed time.

Cave was a good-looking, gentlemanly fellow; quite the most gentlemanly of the travellers, in Mr Parker's opinion, and as a reward to Cave for being so personable and gentlemanly, Mr Parker had several times taken him home to tea; the only traveller he had ever singled out for such distinction. He was sorry for Cave, who had once told him he wasn't very happy with his wife, she was always ailing or something. If it was this last, Mr Parker felt for Cave, because his own wife Flora was always imagining she had something the matter with her nowadays.

Perhaps Cave had gone on his holidays, mused Mr Parker. Though he hadn't said anything about it last time he called. From Cave's holidays, Mr Parker's thoughts passed to his own. They started tomorrow. In his mind's eye, he saw himself sitting in a deck-chair on the sands at Llandudno, reading the paper. He was already in imagination wearing his grey alpaca jacket and his holiday panama. At this time tomorrow, he mused, he would be just about to take his customary walk at the edge of the sea, having first sent Flora indoors with Margaret. He sat with his wife and daughter in the afternoons, but when it grew chilly, Margaret took her mother back to the first-floor front sitting-room at Mrs Bright's.

The Parkers had gone for years to Llandudno and to Mrs Bright's. Mrs Bright knew Mr Parker's ways, Flora explained apologetically, when asked if they were going *again* to Llandudno. Mrs Bright knew exactly how Mr Parker liked the mutton done and she made no objection to preparing a bowl of patent food at half-past ten at night, at which most landladies would certainly have jibbed. So many free samples of patent foods came to the shop that it seemed a pity not to make use of them and Mr Parker had got into the habit of having a bowl of something of that sort every night at half-past ten.

No matter how sleepy his daughter was she had to stay up, at home, to make it for him.

For many years now, Alec had not accompanied his parents and sister to Llandudno. He took more exciting holidays elsewhere and had this year spent a fortnight at Cannes with the senior partner of his firm, Mr Watson, and his family of daughters. The Watsons had further shown their gratifying interest in Alec by inviting him for the two weekends he could not spend at home, since the house was to be closed during the family's absence at Llandudno. Mr Parker was glad in any case to be going to Llandudno, but he was more than ever glad now that his going was the cause of Alec's invitation to visit the Watsons at their home. This certainly was, in the opinion of both father and son, a step up.

So that, on this summer evening, Mr Parker was pretty well satisfied with his life on the whole. There were, of course, some crumpled rose-leaves. There were even some thorns; in any life there always are, but Mr Parker considered himself a philosopher about his. As long as the big things, he told himself, the things that mattered, were all right, you had to accept the small troubles. The things that mattered to him, he thought, were his position in the town, his pleasant relations with his customers, Alec's position and his relations with the Watsons. So long as these remained satisfactory, he must accept the fact, he told himself, that Flora, his wife, was less of a companion and more of an invalid, imaginary, every day, that his daughter Margaret was not half so cheerful as she ought to be, and that his assistant James Butler had no tact, never would have any tact and would continue to be a source of irritation to his employer until the day he gave him the sack. If he hadn't been going on his holiday tomorrow, Mr Parker told himself he might have given him the sack that very afternoon.

He looked sideways now at James Butler standing in the little room off the shop, holding a bottle to the light. His quiff of hair was sticking up as usual. James's quiff annoyed Mr Parker. It was common, he informed James. But no matter how many times James had it cut off, it came again. He told Mr Parker with desperation that it *grew* like that, but Mr Parker did not believe it. The quiff was part of James's general lack of taste and tact, an example of which James had given that very afternoon.

At the time, Mr Parker was himself occupied in the dispensary and James was on duty behind the counter. Someone came into the shop and in a loud, hearty voice – his voice was always much too loud and hearty for his employer's taste – James said: 'Good afternoon, Miss Price, and what can I do for you?'

Miss Price was a timid girl in the Borough Treasurer's office and Mr Parker did not take much interest in her as a rule. But her request to James was so low that Mr Parker's curiosity was piqued and he looked out. Miss Price was on tiptoe, whispering to James over the counter and James, in imitation of Mr Parker, was listening with carefully averted eyes, so as not to embarrass a nervous customer. This was all right. For one moment, Mr Parker cherished a hope that at last James was learning. But this hope was doomed to swift extinction.

'Something to cure perspiration?' bellowed James. 'Half a

minute. I'll just inquire from Mr Parker. Here's Miss Price, Mr Parker,' bellowed James, proceeding to inquire without moving from his place at the counter. 'She wants something to cure perspiration. They call it BO, now, you know, Miss Price,' he finished facetiously.

Mr Parker hurried. With a look at James Butler, he thrust him aside and bent to the deeply-blushing Miss Price.

'Ah, Miss Price,' he said in a voice that was at the same time soothing to her and a lesson to James Butler. 'A most distressing complaint, is it not? You'd be surprised how frequently I am consulted about it. By very refined people too,' said Mr Parker rummaging under the counter. 'I can assure you, Miss Price, that excessive transpiration through the skin is not confined to the working-classes. To the horny handed sons of toil, as it were. Oh, no. Now, I have the very thing here . . .'

'You oaf, James,' said Mr Parker, turning angrily on his assistant when the door closed on Miss Price. 'You tactless oaf, what did you want to shout it out like that for?'

James, his eyebrows up, his quiff of hair up, looked in injured astonishment at his employer. Shout it out? He didn't know that he had shouted it out. Besides, there was nobody in the shop so what did it matter if he had shouted it out? He said so in self-defence, but he only irritated his employer the more. Mr Parker was always angry if James tried to defend himself.

'If a customer whispers, you should whisper too, you clumsy fool. When will you learn that this is a high-class pharmacy and not a Saturday night stall on the market? If it had been anybody but Miss Price, my boy, you'd have got the sack today. And then where would you have been? Where would you have got another job? You, who can't even pass the College of Preceptors. Twenty-two years of age and can't even pass the College of Preceptors.'

James knew Mr Parker would throw this up at him, and, flushing all down the back of his neck, he turned away. He could say nothing more. It was only too true. He had failed the College of Preceptors examination six times before he took it for the seventh time a few weeks ago and the news had just come through that he had failed again. Until he could pass the examination, Mr Parker would continue to taunt him and to withhold a rise in wages, and what was worse, James couldn't propose to Cissy Battersby, with whom he had been walking out for the last twelve months. Cissy Battersby was puzzled, but poor James said nothing in explanation. He did not feel justified in offering himself to her until he had passed the College of Preceptors and got a rise.

When Mr Parker came back from his holiday, James and Cissy would go off together for a week at Blackpool, according to the innocent habit of the betrothed in their walk of life. Courting couples in Sefton and elsewhere went away together for their holidays and nobody thought any evil of them. James would go with Cissy and would spend many anguished hours not being able to say anything about getting married. Mr Parker reminded him of this now and James turned away, silenced, the fight gone out of him.

After incidents of this kind, Mr Parker showed his displeasure by not speaking to James. But today it was difficult to carry this punishment through because he was going away on the morrow and there were instructions to be left for James and for old Mr Snow, who came to dispense the medicines in Mr Parker's absence. He was therefore obliged to speak to James, but he did it with as little movement of the lips as possible, to show that he would not have done it at all unless obliged.

'You must give this order to Cave when he comes. He evidently is not coming today.'

'No, sir,' said James. He only remembered to call his employer 'sir' after being rebuked.

'Did he say anything to you about not coming at his usual time when he called last?'

'No, sir.'

Mr Parker glanced under his eyelids at James. James was properly subdued this time, and so he ought to be.

The Town Hall clock began to strike. Mr Parker went to the window and drew down the blind, to the door, and drew down the blind there. On each, in white letters on the blue linen, was written: 'George E Parker. Major Pharmacist.' Nobody in Sefton knew what that meant, but everybody was suitably impressed.

James came humbly out of the dispensary to bid his employer farewell.

'I hope you enjoy your holiday, sir,' he said.

'Thank you,' said Mr Parker distantly. He wasn't going to forgive James as easily as all that, so James needn't think so. 'I have no doubt,' he added self-righteously, 'that I shall.'

He put on his hat and took a final look round the shop.

'Don't you forget my tomatoes,' he said to James.

'No, sir.'

'You've to come round every day, beginning from tomorrow evening, and remember the key's under a flat stone by the clump of yellow nasturtiums to the left of the door,' he said sternly, his eyes boring into James to discover if James was harbouring any notion of shirking these instructions.

'Very good, sir.'

His tomatoes, reared so carefully by himself in the tiny greenhouse outside the drawing-room windows, were peculiarly precious to Mr Parker. In fact, among the things that really mattered to Mr Parker the tomatoes should earlier have been enumerated. Nothing gave Mr Parker purer pleasure – because his other pleasures were mixed with snobbery – than to watch the formation of a tomato on his plants, to watch it ripen, to sever it at the appointed time, to weigh it in the palm of his hand and above all to smell it. Dearer far to Mr Parker than all the perfumes of Arabia was the smell of a tomato freshly gathered from one of his own plants. It was one of the grudges he secretly bore his wife, that she took no notice of his tomatoes. She never remarked on them. He had long ceased to show them to her.

The year before, while the Parkers were at Llandudno, a disaster had befallen the tomatoes. Someone got into the greenhouse and stole them. When Mr Parker returned home, expectant of a fine crop, there were none. He was horrified. The theft seemed to him so extremely mean. To steal a man's tomatoes! He was determined that this year such a thing should not happen. James Butler was to come round every day, remove the ripe tomatoes and take them to the shop, to store against Mr Parker's return. He was also to keep a sharp look-out for the thief, on whom Mr Parker swore, if he should ever catch him, to have the law.

'You can go away with a quiet mind, Mr Parker,' said James, fishing eagerly for forgiveness. 'I'll look after the tomatoes.'

'Good evening, then,' said Mr Parker, unrelenting to the last.

He went out of the shop. Throwing out his chest and striking the pavement lightly with his stick, he went up the street towards his home, towards his holiday.

II

Anyone who speculated upon Mr Parker's habits and behaviour would have been sure that he must have chosen a respectable neighbourhood to live in; and so he had. The eye of the beholder might see nothing in Lawn Terrace but a row of tall, begrimed houses, with small gardens before and long gardens behind. The beholder might have thought Lawn Terrace both dull and depressing; he could not know that Miss Fanny Martin lived in the double house at the end and redeemed everything.

Miss Martin not only lived in Lawn Terrace, she owned it. Middle-aged and a spinster, without the advantages of youth, beauty and the married state, thought by some to be the sole advantages of the female sex, Miss Fanny was nevertheless a person of consequence and Mr Parker admired her excessively.

His wife and daughter, on the other hand and perhaps in consequence, did not admire Miss Martin at all. They did not say so, even to each other, partly from a sense of loyalty to Mr Parker and partly because they did not say much of anything to each other. Some sort of barrier had grown up between mother and daughter during these last years. Flora sighed over it at times, but thought it couldn't be helped. It all seemed part of growing old, that husband, son and daughter should move away from her.

Flora had rather given up these last few years. She had retired into a semi-invalidism which added interest to her own life, irritation to her husband's and extra work to her daughter's. She was getting into the habit of spending one day a week in bed. She found it most pleasant to sit up in a mauve bed-jacket – she was fond of mauve – and be waited on by Margaret. She had the flowers brought up from the dining-room and placed on the dressing-table and that made her feel quite the invalid. She wished she had thought of this weekly day in bed before; it would have enlivened the years since the children had grown up and away. She spoke of this voluntary retirement to bed as 'my day.'

'I'll have my day on Tuesday,' she would say, as if she laid no claim to the days she spent out of bed at all.

In her younger days, Mrs Parker had not gone much to the shop, but now she was often in it, asking James Butler, when her husband was out of hearing, if he had anything to do her good. She meant in a general way, since she had nothing specific the matter with her. James was obliging, if a little puzzled how to prescribe. One time he would recommend backache pills, another something for the scalp. She took whatever he gave her, saying she would try it.

It was too late, Mr Parker felt, to change or do anything with Flora, but he wished his daughter to model herself as far as possible upon Miss Fanny Martin, and he strove ceaselessly towards that end. The fact that Margaret remained herself and as unlike Miss Martin as possible did not deter him.

His admiration for Miss Fanny had its effect even on Margaret's hats. Mr Parker paid for his daughter's hats and thought he had the right to approve them before purchase. Hat on head, Margaret would advance into the room where her father sat with the paper.

'Will this one do, Father?' she would ask self-consciously. 'May I keep this one?'

Over his paper he would look at it. Unconsciously he looked at it with Miss Fanny's eyes, and if it wasn't the sort of hat Miss Fanny would approve of, Margaret couldn't have it.

He admired Miss Martin's flat hats with bows on, her winter tailor-mades, her summer foulards, her way of talking, her way of walking.

'Why can't you walk like Miss Fanny?' he would ask Margaret. 'You ought to take a lesson from her. She walks like a pheasant.'

Margaret said nothing, but she wondered how she could walk like Miss Fanny who threw out her bust, when she herself had no bust to speak of to throw out. Margaret was twenty-three and slender; Miss Fanny was forty-six and very solid.

Miss Martin was a vigilant guardian of the proprieties in her Terrace. If tea-towels were hung out in the back gardens in the afternoons to dry, Miss Martin sent a note. Tea-towels were allowed in the mornings only. When the people at number five bought a Macaw and put it out on fine days to benefit from the sun, Miss Martin sent a note and it was taken in again. If a chimney smoked, Miss Martin sent a note. If a wireless or gramophone was heard, Miss Martin sent a note. Nobody murmured against this middle-aged martinet, least of all Mr Parker. Mr Parker thought Miss Martin was quite right to be so particular. Living in the vicinity of Miss Martin, he felt he was living up to something, though what that something was he did not precisely formulate.

On this summer evening, Mr Parker opened the front door of Number Seven and hanging hat and stick on the stand that stood like an antlered stag at bay at the back of the hall, he went through the drawing-room to the greenhouse. Coming home at the end of the day's work, he did not go in search of wife or daughter, but to look at his tomatoes. When he had gone over them one by one minutely and with pride, he considered sitting in the drawing-room with the paper. But the room was shrouded in dust-sheets against the departure on the morrow, so he took his paper into the dining-room and sat there.

The paper made uneasy reading. Another crisis was looming up. Mr Parker was heartily tired of these crises, and he wanted to go away for his holiday with a quiet mind, so he tried to keep his eyes from the disquieting parts of the paper.

Flora looked in and went out again, saying in a warning sort of way: 'Father's here, Margaret.'

Margaret came in with a dish for the table, which was set

for the high tea they always had unless Alec was at home. Mr Parker took no notice of either wife or daughter. He had been making himself pleasant at the shop all day; it was an understood thing that he should not continue to do it at home. No one spoke much in the house. In fact, a stranger coming into the Parker home might have concluded that there had just been a row and that the members of the family were not, for the time being, on speaking terms.

This taciturnity had grown on them imperceptibly and for different reasons. Mr Parker had come to feel faintly uncomfortable in the company of his wife and daughter. He didn't know why. He only knew he was happy at the shop, ordering James about and obliging the customers, but as soon as he came home, unless Alec was there, he felt a strong desire to disapprove of everything. Flora was silent from a mixture of stubbornness and lethargy; Margaret from occupation with her own thoughts.

Margaret was dark-haired, grey-eyed, pale and quiet. The first time he had come to the house, Cave, the traveller, had congratulated Mr Parker on his pretty daughter, but Mr Parker took it as a compliment intended obliquely for himself.

'Tea's ready, Father,' said Margaret, setting her father's chair to the table.

He took it and bowed his head over cold salmon and salad, stewed cherries and custard. Grace over, he lifted his hands towards the salmon, but let them fall back to the table, fixing a portentous look on Margaret.

'What is it?' she asked, colour flooding her cheeks, her eyes startled. 'Is anything wrong?'

'Where,' asked Mr Parker coldly, 'are the fish-servers?'

'Oh.' Margaret sprang from the table to the side-board drawer. 'I'm sorry,' she said, bringing them out.

With precise care, Mr Parker divided the fish. Then he spoke again and again with severity.

'Is there,' he said, 'no cucumber?'

'Oh,' said Margaret, jumping from the again. 'I forgot it.'

'With so little to remember,' said her father, 'you should never forget anything.'

He tapped his fingers on the table, waiting.

'Was everything all right at the shop today, George?' asked Flora, to fill the gap until the cucumber should come.

'Much as usual,' replied Mr Parker. 'Except that Cave didn't turn up as expected. It was his day and he hadn't informed me to the contrary.'

'Dear me,' said Flora mildly. 'If he had come, you might have brought him home to tea. He hasn't been for quite a time. There's plenty of salmon too. I expect there'll be a good bit left, and then we'll have to take it away with us. It's too good to waste.'

'This is a specimen of Flora's conversation,' thought Mr Parker. 'She used to have some spirit, but where is it now?'

Margaret brought the sliced cucumber.

'Now perhaps I can begin my tea,' said her father. 'Unless there's something else missing.'

There was not and tea proceeded in silence. Mr Parker ate and read the paper. Flora, her eyes blankly on the window, masticated the salmon. Margaret sat between her parents. Her blush had not subsided, but had fixed a carnation colour on her cheeks, to which she pressed the backs of her hands surreptitiously now and then to cool them.

Through the open windows came the sounds of summer evenings in Lawn Terrace, the rustlings of the dark trees in the gardens, the twitterings of the sparrows, the passing of occasional footsteps in the street.

The cherries were served in due course by Mr Parker and a row of stones bordered the three plates. Once Margaret used to count these to herself: 'This year, next year, sometime, never . . .' to find out if the future held anything for her, anything different. But now she had no need to inquire from the stones. She had cast her own lot. She knew what it was. At the thought of that, she threw a wild look under her lashes at her father, but he was reading the paper and did not see.

Tea over, Mr Parker returned to his chair. Flora sat opposite with her mauve wool. She was getting a new bed-jacket on to her needles in preparation for Llandudno. If fine, she would knit on the sands; if wet, in the rooms.

Mr Parker fidgetted behind his paper. At last he looked round it.

'Are my things ready for tomorrow, Flora?'

'Yes, George,' she said, casting on stitches. 'They are.'

'Are they packed?'

'Yes, George.'

He retired behind his paper. There was nothing further, it appeared, to be said to Flora, but Margaret it now seemed to him was being very slow. What was she doing, hanging over the side-board drawer like that? She could have shut the drawer, taken the tray and gone out to the kitchen long ago.

But now she had turned from the drawer and was standing in a vague way at the window, looking out. As if there was anything to look out at, thought Mr Parker testily. At last he could refrain no longer.

'Hadn't you better be getting on with your work?' he said, stirring restively. 'Instead of leaving everything to the last minute? We have to be off early in the morning.'

Margaret started. She seized the tray and hurried out of the room.

For a while, Mr Parker was able to give his full attention to his paper. Until the evening quiet was broken by the sound of a voice, a loud, well-modulated voice, consciously used. Behind his paper, Mr Parker listened, and over her knitting, Flora listened too. Miss Martin was speaking to someone lower down the terrace. Smiling, Mr Parker rose and left the room. Flora, raising an expressionless face, watched him go. In a moment, she heard them conversing over the garden gate.

'Good evening, Miss Martin.'

'There he goes,' thought Flora.

'Ah, good evening, Mr Parker,' fluted Miss Fanny. 'A lovely evening, is it not?'

'It is, indeed.' When George spoke to Miss Martin he tried to speak like her, noted Flora. 'It promises well for my holiday, does it not? We go tomorrow, you know.'

'Do you indeed? And to Llandudno, I presume?'

'To Llandudno,' admitted Mr Parker. 'First thing in the morning. By nine o'clock we shall have left the house.'

'I haven't been away yet,' said Miss Martin. 'I shall take a holiday somewhere abroad later, I fancy.'

'My son went abroad. He went to Cannes this year,' said Mr Parker, getting it in.

'I never go away in August,' said Miss Martin. 'It's such a vulgar month. Everywhere is so vulgar in August.'

'Ah, yes, well . . .' George hummed and hawed uneasily. It had never occurred to him before that August was vulgar. He had *chosen* August. He had always looked upon August as the height of the season. But now Miss Fanny said it was vulgar. He thought of a way of redeeming himself.

'My son won't go away in August,' he said eagerly. 'He always takes his holiday in July. As I say, he went to Cannes with Mr Watson, the senior partner of his firm, who takes a great interest in him.'

'So your house will be closed from tomorrow?' said Miss Martin, ignoring Alec, Cannes and Mr Watson's interest.

'Yes,' said Mr Parker. 'From tomorrow. For a fortnight.'

'Ah, well,' said Miss Martin. 'I hope you enjoy your holiday, Mr Parker. Well-earned, I am sure,' she conceded graciously. '*Good* evening.'

'Good evening, Miss Martin,' said Mr Parker. 'And thank you.'

'What for?' Flora asked herself, turning her needles.

Mr Parker, smiling still, returned to the dining-room. He was disinclined, however, to return to his paper and wished to do something more active. He therefore set about the pleasurable task of addressing the labels for the holiday luggage. He liked writing, so he wrote them all; his own, Flora's, Margaret's.

'Where's your case?' he asked, taking Margaret's label

into the kitchen. 'I suppose it's ready to come down into the hall.'

Margaret, putting the plates away, looked over her shoulder with a startled air. He wished she wouldn't look at him like that; as if he were going to bite her.

'No, Father,' she said. 'It isn't ready yet.'

'Well, why isn't it?' he blustered. 'It ought to be. Nothing to do all day but pack for a holiday and you can't even do that. You'd better go and pack now and bring the case down into the hall with the others.'

Margaret looked away, uncertainly.

'I've a lot of ironing to do for Mother yet,' she said. 'The things must air. I ought to do them now.'

'Well, it's very bad management,' said her father.

He stood for a moment.

'You'll have to tie your own label on then, that's all,' he said. He laid it down and went in displeasure out of the kitchen.

Margaret ironed, transferring lace fronts, boudoir caps, bed-jackets from the table to the clothes-horse before the fire. Daylight died away. Margaret was a shadow moving among shadows.

Before she could finish, her father appeared again.

'If you don't go to bed,' he said severely. 'You'll never be up in the morning. Tea at seven sharp, remember. We've got to be out of the house by nine. You can make my food now,' he permitted.

Margaret stood at the gas-stove, stirring the patent food. She carried it to her father, said good night to her parents and shut them into the dining-room. When the ironing was done, she went upstairs. But when her parents went up in their turn, a line of light still showed under her door.

'Margaret,' cried her father, rapping on her door. 'What are you doing?'

There was silence.

'Margaret! Do you hear me? What are you doing at this time of night?'

Her voice came after a further pause.

'Getting ready for tomorrow, Father.'

'Well, put that light out,' he said. 'It's ridiculous, fiddling about till this time of night.'

He went into his own room and closed the door. But before he got into bed, he looked out again. She had obeyed him. The landing was dark. He could retire in peace.

It was night in Lawn Terrace. Lamplight shone through the leaves of the trees, giving them a beauty they no longer had by day. The houses stood in a solid dark row, their gates closed to the empty street. At Number Seven, the trunk, the cases, the hat-box containing among other hats Mr Parker's panama, waited, labelled, in the hall. In the kitchen, Flora's lace fronts and caps dangled over the clothes-horse to air until the last possible minute, so afraid was she of putting on anything that might be damp. Contrary to her father's instructions, Margaret's case had not been brought down into the hall. Moreover, after darkness and silence had been for some time established, the line of light reappeared under her door.

III

Mr Parker woke to the sound of a dog barking at a distance. For a moment he thought he was at Llandudno. It seemed that the tide must be out and the dog barking at the edge of the sea early on the fine summer morning. But opening his eyes, he realized that he was not at Llandudno. Not yet. He soon would be. But for the present he was still at home in his familiar bed, with Flora beside him. He could see no more of her than the heave of shoulder and hip and the back of one of her boudoir caps buried in the pillow. Margaret would soon be coming in with the tea. He lay pleasantly relaxed, waiting.

The room was furnished with a large, lustrous suite in mahogany inlaid with lover's knots in yellow. The oval mirrors in dressing-table and wardrobe reflected the mauve sweet peas of the wallpaper and the monstrous purple coils of the eider-down, over which, so puffed-up was it, the occupants of the bed could neither see or be seen. Mr Parker pressed down the eiderdown now to look over it at the time.

His pleasant mood was instantly banished. It was five-past seven. The tea should have been in five minutes ago. Unpunctuality, either at the shop or at the house, Mr Parker told himself he would not tolerate. He reached up and pressed the hanging bell long and hard. Sinking back to the pillow, he kept his head turned to the door, frowning in readiness for Margaret to appear. But she did not appear, and in a moment, Mr Parker rose again and pressed the bell more violently than before. He could hear it himself, ringing downstairs in the kitchen. Where was she? What on earth was she doing to be late on the morning they were going away? She knew they had to be out of the house at nine. She knew he always gave himself three-quarters of an hour for shaving and dressing and that Flora took longer. As time went on, Flora took longer and longer. He often thought, with irritation, that soon she would only get herself dressed in time to get undressed again for bed at night.

The bell had been ringing all this time and still Margaret had not appeared. What on earth . . . fumed Mr Parker, throwing his thin legs out of bed and thrusting his arms into his dressing-gown.

'Margaret,' he called over the stairs. 'Margaret? What are you thinking of? The tea is ten minutes late. *Ten minutes,*' he called out.

There was no answer. Leaning over, he could see the kitchen door standing open. Wide open, and there was no sound.

Gathering his dressing-gown about him, Mr Parker hurried down the stairs.

'Margaret,' he said angrily, going forward.

The kitchen was empty, chill, silent. No kettle steamed on the gas-stove, no tray stood prepared. Mr Parker looked about him in an amazement which quickly turned to anger. She wasn't up. She had overslept. Overslept. This morning of all mornings.

He hurried back upstairs and knocked on her door.

'Margaret.'

There was no answer.

'Margaret!'

He laid his ear to the door. A deep sense of propriety kept him from going into his daughter's room. He would not have dreamt of doing such a thing in ordinary circumstances, but the circumstances were not ordinary. He was going to be made late for the train. He opened the door. The room was empty, the bed made.

'Flora,' said Mr Parker, hurrying to his recumbent spouse. 'D'you know that Margaret isn't either upstairs or down? Where is she? The kettle isn't on. I went into her room. She isn't there, but her bed's made.'

Flora raised her head from her comfortable pillow.

'Not there?' she repeated sleepily. 'Dear me, is there no tea yet? I'm ready for my tea. I've had a bad night.'

Mr Parker ignored her night.

'D'you hear what I'm saying?' he asked sternly. 'Margaret isn't in her room and the bed's made.'

'She's probably made it to save time later,' said Flora. 'She's perhaps run out for something. Butter or something. I heard her say we hadn't much.'

'Butter!' ejaculated Mr Parker with scorn for Flora's intelligence. 'What shop is open for the sale of butter at this time in the morning?'

'Perhaps she's gone to borrow some then,' suggested Flora. 'From the Bagshaws or somewhere.'

'Well, if she has, it's disgraceful bad management,' said Mr Parker. 'I suppose I'll have to put the kettle on myself. As for you, you'd better get up and see to the breakfast yourself for a change. We're going to be thrown very late and you know how I dislike that.'

He hurried away and Flora, sighing, slowly heaved herself out of bed. As she crossed the landing on her way to the bathroom, something in the tidy emptiness of the room behind Margaret's open door arrested her. She went in.

A moment later, Mr Parker in the kitchen was startled by a loud cry from the stairs.

'George! George!'

He ran. Flora was standing at the top of the staircase, her face distorted, a sheet of notepaper in her hand.

'George! She's gone. She's gone with that man. That Mr Cave, the traveller. Frank, she calls him. Frank! Oh, she's gone. And didn't you say he was married? Oh, married!'

'Cave? She's gone with Cave?' Mr Parker stood, gazing upwards with his mouth open. His hand was on the rail, his foot on the stair, but he could not move.

'What did you say?' he brought out at last in a strange, loud voice.

'See, George, see for yourself,' Flora stumbled down the stairs to him. 'Oh, I always thought she was such a good, quiet girl with not a thought in her head about men. To deceive us like this! To go with a married man. She must have been meeting him in the afternoons while I was lying down. He's not been to the house above half a dozen times, I'm sure. Oh, George, whyever did you bring him home? You might have known. A blackguard like that.'

'Hold your tongue,' said Mr Parker sternly, trying to read the letter.

But Flora sank sobbing to the stairs and he had to get away from her. He took the letter into the kitchen and started again.

The letter was a long one, but though his eyes ran over it from beginning to end, he could not grasp much of it at once. She had gone with Cave. That was what he grasped. Gone.

Standing in the kitchen with his thin neck and small bald head rising from the cowl-like collar of his Jaeger dressing-gown, he looked like a stricken vulture. Cave. The viper! The only traveller he had ever brought home to tea and this was how he was repaid.

Behind him, the kettle he had put on the gas-stove now boiled all over the floor. He did not notice it.

He read the letter again. See! She knew he was married. She said so. She said he was as unhappy at home as she was. They were both so unhappy they were going away to try to find happiness together. She said she knew they would be outcasts from society, but they would be together. The world would be well lost for love, she said.

Unhappy at home! She said she was unhappy at home. It was the first he'd heard about it, thought her father.

She had gone. Gone with a married man nearly twice her age, disgracing herself and her family. It was the last quarter from which he had expected trouble. Sons sometimes gave trouble; no one expected daughters to. But she had brought down the whole fabric of his tidy, respectable life. Unseen, unheard by anyone but himself, it was crashing about him in ruins.

Flora came weeping into the kitchen and sat down at the table.

'George, George, what are we going to do?'

He took no notice of her. The trouble seemed all his own.

By and by, Flora got up and turned off the gas under the kettle. Mr Parker moved at last.

'I'd better go and get dressed,' he said heavily.

'We've missed that train,' said Flora. 'But I suppose we're not going now.'

'No,' said Mr Parker. 'What should we do at Llandudno now?'

Flora had no answer.

He went out of the kitchen, but halfway up the stairs, he turned and came back again.

'Flora,' he said, 'we're not going away, but it must look as if we've gone. The house must still look closed. No one must get a hint of what's happened. Don't pull up the blinds, don't open the windows or doors. Keep out of sight. Don't light a fire in the kitchen. Smoke would be seen coming out of the chimney.'

Flora stared out of her swollen eyes in amazement.

'If Miss Martin saw we hadn't gone away this morning as we intended, she'd be round at once to find out why. And what could we say?' he asked. 'I'd rather die than let Miss Martin know what's happened,' he said vehemently. 'Or anybody else, either.'

'But George,' said Flora. 'It'll have to come out sometime. Margaret says she's never coming back. She says she realises that we'll never want to see her again,' quavered Flora, her chin quivering. 'It's bound to come out sooner or later.'

'I'll keep it from them as long as possible,' said Mr Parker grimly.

He went out of the kitchen, but again returned.

'I shall ring up Alec by and by. I'll give him time to get to the office. He'll tell us what to do. He'll come over and help us. Thank God we've got Alec. He'd never have disgraced his family like this,' he said bitterly.

'Oh, George, don't talk like that,' wept Flora. 'Poor Margaret. She doesn't know what she's done.'

Feeling old, stricken, Mr Parker began to climb the stairs to get dressed. And as he climbed, there came the slow boom of the Town Hall clock striking nine. They might all have been off to Llandudno by now.

IV

Even in distress, Mr Parker was discreet. He cupped the mouthpiece of the telephone in his hand and spoke into it out of the side of his mouth.

'Alec? Is that you, Alec?'

'Yes?' Alec's voice, cool, even cold, came from Liverpool. 'Is that you, Father?'

'Yes, Alec.'

'What's the matter? I'm very occupied at this time in the morning, you know, opening the letters,' said Alec importantly.

'It's urgent, Alec, or I wouldn't have rung you up.'

'Well, what is it? I thought you'd gone to Llandudno.'

'That's just it, Alec. We can't go.'

'Why?'

'Well, Alec, I can hardly bring myself to tell you.'

'I wish you would,' said Alec tersely. 'I'm pressed for time.'

'Well, it's this, Alec . . .'

There was a silence.

'Margaret's run away from home,' he whispered.

'She's run away with Cave. The traveller. For Scorseby's, you know. He's a married man, Alec. When we got up this morning, we found she'd gone, leaving a letter . . .'

'Wait a minute, Father. Let's get this clear. Do I understand you to say that she has gone off with a *traveller*?'

'Yes, Alec. A married man.'

There was silence on the telephone. Then Alec's voice came in deep disgust.

'A *traveller*. My God.'

Another silence.

Then his voice came again.

'If it had been a gentleman, I might have understood it. But a *commercial*!'

Strangely enough this aspect of the situation had not struck Mr Parker. But he hastened now to agree.

'Yes, Alec,' he said. 'It's awful, isn't it?'

'Awful,' said Alec.

There was another silence.

'This'll make nice news for the Watsons, won't it?' said Alec bitterly.

His father, wretched, did not answer.

'I shan't tell them,' said Alec.

'No,' said Mr Parker. 'It would be better not. It's not a thing we want to tell anybody.'

Another silence. Then Mr Parker spoke again.

'I don't know what to do, Alec. I don't know what to do for the best.'

'There's nothing to be done,' said Alec. 'She's gone away,

she'll have to stop away. You don't know where she's gone, I suppose?'

'No. She didn't say. She said she was never coming back.'

'It's to be hoped she doesn't. It's bad enough to go,' said Alec. 'But it would be worse to come back.'

Mr Parker considered this in silence.

'But we can't leave it at that,' he said at last. 'Cave's no good and he's twice as old as she is. What sort of a life can she live with him?'

'She should have thought of that before she went,' said Alec coldly.

'Well,' he said after another pause, 'we'll have to keep this dark, as far as I am concerned. Mr Watson doesn't like scandals. Not in the firm.'

'I thought you and I would go after them, Alec. Try and find out where they've gone and get her back,' said Mr Parker.

'What would be the good of that?' asked Alec. 'She's of age. Besides, she's done for herself. Going off with a married man. A traveller, too. You'd better let her drop out of sight now. As for me, Father, I can't let myself be drawn into this sort of thing. I can't go chasing a runaway pair about the place, you know. It's not the thing for a man in my position. Besides, it's such a sordid affair. I don't want to have anything to do with it.'

Another pause.

'Will you come over, Alec?' said Mr Parker. 'It's difficult to talk on the telephone, and we're stuck here in this house. We don't want the neighbours to know we haven't gone away.'

'But you should go away,' said Alec. 'Llandudno's the best place for you. There's no point in stopping at home.'

'We shan't go away, Alec,' said his father with sudden firmness. 'Will you come over?'

'I'm afraid I can't manage it, Father. Not today. We're very busy, and I'm dining at the Watsons. As a matter of fact, I've made up my mind to propose to Daphne Watson tonight. That's why I'm so upset at what Margaret has done. Running off with a commercial traveller! She might have thought of other people before she did a thing like that. Nice sister-in-law for Daphne, isn't she? It's enough to make Daphne refuse me. But I shan't tell her. Not yet, anyway. So you see, Father, I've too much of my own on hand to come over just at present. There's no point in coming over, either. I've nothing further to say. I've told you what I think you ought to do. Leave Margaret to go her own way; she's chosen it. And you go to Llandudno. Now there are the pips going again. You've had three calls already. You ring off and go to Llandudno. Mother all right? If you write to me, be sure to put personal on the envelope. I don't want anything opened in the General Office. I shall have to say goodbye. I hear Mr Watson coming in. Goodbye.'

'Goodbye,' said Mr Parker.

He replaced the receiver and sat slumped before the telephone, staring grimly before him.

Flora came into the room.

'Isn't he coming?'

She asked, but she seemed to know he wasn't.

Mr Parker shook his head. He got up and went out of the room. He kept doing that. Every time Flora came into a room where he was, he left it. They were no comfort to each other.

They had lost the habit of sharing anything and they could not share trouble now.

Mr Parker went upstairs and stood in the bedroom in the bluish gloom made by the lowered blinds. He took Margaret's letter from his pocket and peered at it again. After reading, he stared away from it. He was staggered, he told himself. Completely staggered.

Standing in the shrouded room with its unmade bed and general dishevelment left over from the night, Mr Parker suffered a great revulsion of feeling, a revulsion against his life, which only yesterday had seemed so satisfactory. Everything was ugly. Everything had gone wrong. Everything. Margaret had ruined herself and him, Alec had failed him. With sudden bitter clarity, Mr Parker knew that there was nothing to be expected from Alec, either now or at any other time. He had striven to elevate Alec and Alec was so elevated that before long he would pass clean out of his father's sight.

As for Margaret, he was vague about what he ought to have done, but he felt guiltily that he hadn't done it. It did not exactly occur to Mr Parker that he was reaping as he had sown. Few of us get as far as that. But he did wonder if his treatment of his children had been wrong. The one he had spoiled had failed him, the one he had neglected had run away from him and so he had lost them both.

Self-revelation was so painful and unusual to Mr Parker that he swerved away from it. He sought for someone else to blame, he sought for a scapegoat and found Flora. Flora was as much to blame as he was. More. She was Margaret's mother, Margaret's proper guardian. But what had she ever done for

Margaret except let her wait on her? Flora was so lazy and self-indulgent . . .

Here the scapegoat came into the room, sighing, to make the bed and Mr Parker, lest he should burst out with what he was thinking, plunged down the stairs again to seek another refuge.

Flora's sighs had re-echoed through the house all the morning. She went heavily about doing things she hadn't done for years and finding them very hard work. All the time she was washing-up, mopping floors, dusting furniture, she longed to have finished and sit down. But when she sat down for a few moments to rest, it was far worse than working, so she got up and went on again, in spite of her tired legs.

When she had finished making the bed, she, in her turn, stood in the bluish gloom, and in her turn, she suffered a revulsion of spirit. What a life, she thought, and what a life it's going to be now, alone in this house with George, and Margaret gone. Oh, I didn't realize until now, she thought, how much she did for me.

In the midst of her distress, she nevertheless became aware that someone had opened the front garden gate and was coming up the path. Wiping her eyes, Flora went to the window and peeped through the blind. Unhappy though she was, she could still feel indignant. Miss Fanny Martin was standing in the garden, looking about her.

'She thinks we're away, so she comes in to get a better look round than she could get if we were at home,' said Flora to herself. 'I knew she was that sort of Nosey Parker.'

Her husband came into the room and Flora dropped the

blind with a start. The worst of George was that he always came on the scene when you least wished him to.

'Come away from that blind,' he hissed, rushing at her like a little bull. 'What on earth are you doing?'

'I'm looking to see what Miss Martin wants in our front garden,' said Flora defiantly.

'Miss Martin!' Already pale in the ghastly blue light, Mr Parker went paler. 'D'you mean to say Miss Martin's down there? In the garden?'

'Yes,' said Flora. 'Having a look round, though what at, I don't know.'

'And you go looking through the blind at her? When you *know* that's she's the very person we want to keep this from? Flora, come out of this room. You're not to be trusted. You're simply not to be trusted,' he said, pushing ineffectually at Flora's large person.

'Oh, what difference does it make?' said Flora, as if he made her tired. 'What good is it doing us or anybody else shutting us up in the house like this? You're always thinking of your precious Miss Martin. Besides,' she charged suddenly, reaching the landing and turning on him, 'it's all your fault.'

'My fault?' he said. 'What's my fault?'

'Everything,' said Flora recklessly. 'You've driven Margaret away.'

'I've driven Margaret away?' cried Mr Parker.

'Yes, you,' said Flora. 'You and your ways.'

'My ways?' he echoed.

What on earth did she mean by his ways? He hadn't any.

'What precisely do you mean by my ways, Flora?' he asked stiffly.

'Oh, I can't describe them,' said Flora wearily. 'I only know they knocked all the stuffing out of me long ago.'

'Knocked all the stuffing out of you! What on earth do you mean by that vulgarity, pray? It is one of the things that makes you so trying to live with, Flora, that you have such difficulty in expressing yourself with propriety.'

'There you are,' said Flora. 'That's one of your ways.'

Mr Parker glared. Then he counter-charged.

'As if it isn't *you*,' he said in a strangled voice. 'As if it isn't you who've driven Margaret away, if anybody has. You've got so lazy these last years, you've never thought of anybody but yourself. Margaret, me, the house, anybody, anything, could go wrong. You'd never have tried to stop it. You imply that I find fault, that I'm over-critical. Well, I may have been, but it's because I knew you'd never do anything in that way. I've had to do the work of two parents. You've left it to me to bring the children up.'

'And a poor job you've made of it,' said Flora.

He wished he wasn't a man with high principles, because he longed to hit her. The most unrespectable emotions seethed within him as he stood on the landing with Flora – Margaret's door wide and accusing between them.

'You,' he gulped. 'You've shirked everything. You've spent your time pampering yourself, lying down, eating sweets, having days in bed . . .'

'Oh,' cried Flora, aghast. 'Speaking to me like that! Me – with my bad health!'

'Gar,' said Mr Parker, vulgar now himself. 'Your health's not bad and you know it. You sleep sound every night of your life and what's more, you snore. You're a fat, lazy woman and you've left all the work to Margaret and let yourself go to pieces.'

'George!'

Flora gaped at him in terror. He was saying such dreadful things. Things she had tried to keep from herself.

'It's true,' he said bitterly. 'You never think of anybody but yourself. You never take any *part*.'

'That's your fault,' said Flora rallying. 'You fuss so much, I do just the opposite. I decided long ago to do just the opposite. You say you find fault because I never do. Well, I never find fault because you always do. So there you are. It's your fault after all.'

They were launched now on such a quarrel as they had not had since the days of their hot youth. They had not felt anything for each other for a long time, but now they felt burning anger, horror, astonishment to hear what each thought of the other. And they brought out everything they had been piling up against each other for years. She even brought out Miss Martin and he brought out his tomatoes.

'You never take any interest in anything I do,' he charged her. 'You never take any interest in my tomatoes. Never.'

'Tomatoes!' Flora laughed and sobbed into her handkerchief. 'Fancy bringing up a thing like tomatoes! As if anyone with any sense could be hurt about tomatoes. It shows what a soft thing you are.'

'Miss Fanny!' he said scornfully, when she told him she was

sick of having Miss Fanny quoted at her and so was Margaret. It was one of the things that made Margaret unhappy at home, she knew, that everlasting holding-up of Miss Fanny. And no wonder.

'It's absolutely ridiculous,' defended Mr Parker. 'Miss Fanny! I admire her, that's all. She's a lady. And *she's* not let herself go to pieces . . .'

'There you go again,' said Flora.

It was a dreadful quarrel. It went on and on. In the end they could find nothing more to say. They had said everything. Weeping, Flora pushed past George and went into the bedroom, locking the door.

Mr Parker, seething still, went downstairs. To think he had lived all these years with someone who thought as badly of him as that! He was considerably shaken and it was some time before he could compose himself sufficiently to put through a trunk call to Scorseby's, the manufacturing chemists.

When it came to speaking to them on the telephone, he found it difficult to ask where Cave had gone without disclosing the fact that his daughter had gone with him. His questions were so cautious that they did not receive the answers he wanted. All that he could find out was that Cave hadn't called at his shop as usual because he had changed his district and was now travelling another.

'He hasn't left you, then?' ventured Mr Parker.

'Oh, no,' said the voice at the other end of the wire. 'But our Mr Begbie will be calling upon you in the course of a day or so. In the meantime, if there is anything urgent, I shall be only too pleased to take your order now.'

Mr Parker stammered his way out of this and asked for Cave's home address. After a long wait, it was given to him. Mon Repos, Rosecroft Avenue, Westley-on-Sea.

'I thought he lived at Warrington,' exclaimed Mr Parker.

'He moved recently,' said the voice, rather coldly, implying that enough time had been spent on something that wasn't business.

Mr Parker rang off. He had Cave's home address, but he didn't know what good it was to him. Cave had left home. And it was not likely that he had left his address with the wife he had deserted. Mr Parker sat on at the table feeling helpless.

The day was interminable. It was the strangest the Parkers had ever spent. Outside the sun shone bright, the sparrows twittered, people went about. But George and Flora remained hidden in the house, withdrawn, shut up with their own selves and with each other. And for each the other was like a guilty conscience, a reminder of shortcomings.

For lunch, Flora laid yesterday's left-over salmon before George. She made tea for herself and carried it upstairs to drink in solitude. Since George disliked her so much, she would keep out of his way.

But by the end of the afternoon, she could stand solitude no longer. She went into the drawing-room where George was sitting with yesterday's paper and said:

'We want some milk. Hadn't you better telephone to James Butler to make sure that he is coming here this evening?'

'No,' he said shortly. 'I hadn't.'

'Why?'

Mr Parker looked at her. He wasn't used to being asked why.

He marvelled at the rapid change that was taking place in Flora. Yesterday she had been lethargic, unquestioning; now she was rude, hostile, critical.

'Why can't you telephone?' she persisted.

'Because Mr Snow might answer the telephone, and I'm supposed to be in Llandudno. I suppose you hadn't thought of that?' he said. 'But I had. I've thought of everything.'

'You've thought too much. You should be doing something,' said Flora, going out of the room.

Mr Parker swallowed anger and sat on. The blinds were only half down in the drawing-room and he could see out without being seen. His eyes travelled continually from the clock on the mantelpiece to the door at the end of the garden through which James, if he were coming, would come. He wondered if James would come, if he would obey instructions when he thought his employer could not know whether he obeyed them or not. Or would James fail him too?

The Town Hall clock struck six. The shop would be closing. What a lifetime had passed since he closed it himself last night!

He waited. Before the finger of the clock on the mantelpiece could get round to the half-hour, the door at the bottom of the garden opened and James appeared. Mr Parker, exhausted by all that had happened to him, was in a weakened mood and tears pricked his eyes to find James faithful.

He felt a pang of self-reproach, too, to note how different was James's demeanour when he fancied himself free of his employer's critical observation. His hat was on the back of his head, his quiff of hair stood up unimpeded, his hands

146

were in his pockets, he whistled; he looked care-free, buoyant. He came up the garden-path, bent to the clump of yellow nasturtiums for the key, unlocked the greenhouse door and went inside, where he surveyed with admiration the tomatoes.

But as he surveyed, it seemed to him that a face took form behind them. James's gaze became stony with fear. It seemed to him that the face of his employer hovered in the gloom of the room behind the greenhouse. A chill went over him, the hair rose still higher on his head. The face came nearer, showed clearer. A hand beckoned. The door between the drawing-room and the greenhouse opened and Mr Parker drew the shaken James within.

'It *is* you, then, Mr Parker? You *are* here?'

'Yes, James, I'm here. I'm glad you've come, James. Good lad. Sh, now, keep quiet. Come and sit down at the back of the room with me, where we can't be seen.'

'Why, whatever is it, Mr Parker?' whispered James in alarm. 'You've not had a death in the family, have you?'

'No,' said Mr Parker. 'Worse.'

'Worse?' exclaimed James.

'Sit down, James,' said Mr Parker, pushing James into one shrouded chair and taking another himself. 'I shall have to tell you what I'd hesitate to tell my best friend. If I had one.'

He rubbed his knees for a time in silence. It was painful to him to reveal a family disgrace to one he had snubbed and bullied and generally taken it out of in the shop. James Butler felt this.

'Don't tell me if you'd rather not, Mr Parker,' he said. 'Can't I help, like, without you having to tell me?'

Mr Parker shook his head, but the suggestion helped him to begin. He got it out. About Margaret. About Cave.

James's candid face changed from amazement to deep gravity as he listened.

'I never liked that chap,' he said, when Mr Parker had finished. 'She's been taken in by him. He tells lies, does that chap. I wouldn't trust him a yard. I never could understand why you took a fancy to him, Mr Parker,' said James, making his employer wince. 'And I bet his hair's permed. Eh, it's a bad business. Can't you go after her and get her back?'

'How?' asked Mr Parker desperately. 'I've been thinking all day. I don't know what to do. I can't set the police on to him. Everybody'd know then. Besides, she's of age. I've no control over her legally. She's gone with her eyes open. She knows he's married. I don't know where they've gone to. I rang up Scorseby's and got his home address, but what's the good of that since he's left home? He'd moved to Westley-on-Sea, they tell me.'

'I thought he lived in Warrington,' said James.

'He's moved.'

'When did he move?'

'They said recently.'

'Oh,' said James. 'Then happen he's left his wife in Warrington and set up with your daughter in Westley. It wouldn't be the first time a commercial's done that.'

Mr Parker winced.

'But he'd never give that address to his firm in that case,' he objected.

'He'd have to give them an address they could find him at,'

said James. 'And if he's set up with your daughter permanently . . .' Seeing his employer wince again, James altered without improving it. 'Well, let's say if he's set up with her just for the time being, that's the address he'd give 'em. The address where he lived or intended to live. That's what I think, anyway.'

Mr Parker rose and plunged to the drawer in the writing-desk.

'I could get there tonight,' he said, bringing out a timetable. 'It's not more than an hour and a half by train. By Jove, James, I'll go. I'll just get the seven-five. Let yourself out this way, will you? Don't bother about the tomatoes. I'll see to them myself. Put the key back in its old place on the hook under the window. Come in tomorrow on your way down, there's a good lad. I may need you again. Goodbye. I'm glad you thought of this, James. It makes me feel I'm doing something, even though nothing may come of it.'

'Flora,' he shouted, rushing out into the hall. 'I'm catching the seven-five to Westley. Margaret may be there. I don't know when I'll be back, but sometime in the middle of the night.'

'I'm coming with you,' said Flora.

Mr Parker, his arms halfway into the sleeves of his summer coat, stared at her.

'You're what?' he said.

'I'm coming with you,' repeated Flora, hurrying with surprising agility up the stairs.

'You can't, Flora,' said Mr Parker. 'I've got to hurry. You know you can't hurry. You never hurry.'

'I can hurry when I have to,' said Flora, reappearing fully

dressed for the street. He didn't know how she'd done it in the time. As for him he couldn't find his hat.

'When there's something to hurry for, I can hurry,' said Flora, hurrying to the front door.

'Not that way,' cried her husband, pulling her back.

'Dear me, I forgot,' she said.

This admission somehow mollified Mr Parker. We are all sensitive instruments played upon by each other. Mr Parker was more than usually overstrung by the shocks and quarrels of the morning and Flora had struck some loud, painful discords out of him. But this gentler touch, inadvertent or not, brought strange relief. Much of the irritation left Mr Parker's face, leaving it merely pathetically harassed. Although he did not feel better about his daughter's disappearance, he looked better; that is, he looked more likeable and Flora, in her turn, responded to that.

They left by the garden door and hurried silently down the back alley. The town was quiet at this hour, business being over and pleasure going on in other parts, in the outskirts, the open spaces, the Corporation Park where the band was playing. Mr Parker kept a sharp look-out for customers, so that he could avoid them. Once he had gone out of his way to salute customers in the street, but not now. He thanked heaven they were high-class customers and as such mostly at dinner.

They reached the station by devious routes and in time. Waiting on the platform, they withdrew behind a stack of wooden boxes. When the train came, they slipped into it like criminals making a get-away.

Westley lay almost unnoticeable between sea and sky; it lay flat, on a flat shore, like a place that has thrown itself face downwards at the edge of the sea, and the new housing estate to which the taxi bore George and Flora Parker was like a child's game on the sands: little houses, toy gardens, no trees and mellifluous names to the roads. The Parkers looked with painful interest through the taxi windows. Was she here? Was this the place the man had brought her to?

'When you get to Rosecroft Avenue,' said Mr Parker sternly to the driver. 'Stop at one end or the other, I don't care which. But don't go into it.'

'Right,' said the driver indifferently. The agitation of his fares was nothing to him.

'Now, Flora,' pleaded Mr Parker. He found it safer now to plead than to command. 'I'd like to manage this business myself. I'd like to go to the house by myself, if you don't mind.'

'All right,' permitted Flora. 'I'll wait about.'

'Thank you,' said Mr Parker.

'Here you are,' said the driver.

They alighted. Mr Parker paid the driver and watched him out of sight. He wasn't going to have the man knowing what he had come to do in Rosecroft Avenue.

'You wait here, Flora,' he said.

Flora nodded and took up her stance at the corner, a bulky figure clasping a bag. She watched him go up the road, proceeding from gate to gate, grasping each gate and peering up each front garden to read the name of the house, painted, mostly, on a sign swinging over the porch. The front gardens were long and Mr Parker's eyes were not very good, so his progress was slow as he went halting and peering up the avenue.

Then all at once, Flora knew, by the tautness of his outline, that he had come to the house. In the evening quiet, she heard the latch of the gate under his hand. He disappeared from her view and she stood waiting.

Mr Parker went up the path between the unfinished garden-beds. The tenant of the house had evidently not been long in occupation. At the porch, Mr Parker pulled up. He had thought of throwing the door open, going straight in and catching them unawares. But faced with the flimsy, but infrangible barrier of an Englishman's front door, he daren't carry out his plan. He thought he ought to ring. So he rang, and standing on the porch, clasped his hands to steady them and kept his eyes on the door that would presently open.

A woman's light steps approached. Mr Parker grew rigid. The door opened, but it was not Margaret who opened it. It was a much older woman, prettyish, with an unsuitably childish ribbon tying up a cloud of faded fair hair. She stood with her head on one side in inquiry, smiling, She smiled. She didn't look in the least like a deserted wife. Mr Parker was overcome with doubt. Perhaps she wasn't. Perhaps he had come to the wrong house. He looked at the sign above his head again. Mon Repos, it said firmly.

'Is this Mr Cave's house?' he asked.

'That's right,' said the woman pleasantly. 'But he's not at home. I'm Mrs Cave. Can I give a message?'

'You're Mrs Cave?' said Mr Parker. In the dusk she could not see his piercing gaze.

'That's right,' she said. 'Can I give him any message?'

Mr Parker concealed his amazement.

'Do you *expect* to be able to give him any message?' he asked, significantly.

'Oh, yes,' I can give him a message when he comes home on Friday.'

'Ah,' said Mr Parker, staring at her. 'When he comes home on Friday.'

He paused. The woman rattled the door-handle with some impatience.

'I was just listening to the news,' she said.

Mr Parker continued to stare.

'You expect your husband home on Friday then?' he said.

'That's right,' said Mrs Cave. 'He always comes home on Friday.'

'And you think he'll be home on Friday this week as usual?'

'I know he will,' said Mrs Cave. 'I had a postcard this morning to say so, too. Where is it? It's here,' she said, reaching behind her to the hall table. '"Home on Friday as usual," it says. So if you want to see him you'd better come back then.'

'You say I can see him if I come back on Friday?' he said.

'That's right,' said Mrs Cave, trying to shut the door.

'What time?' he asked.

'Oh, half-past five time or something like that,' said Mrs Cave.

'Thank you,' said Mr Parker, hurrying off in case she should change it.

'What name?' Mrs Cave called after him. But as he did not reply, she did not call again, but shut the door to hurry back to the news.

VI

It was two tired, disappointed, puzzled people who let themselves into the house in Lawn Terrace after midnight that night. They opened the door and came into the stale, empty house and when they switched on the light in the kitchen, each was startled by the wan face of the other. They were being much kinder to each other now. George helped Flora off with her coat and she stood at the gas-stove on her painful feet to make his patent-food, although he protested that he didn't want it. She made tea for herself, but did not carry it into a separate place to drink it this time. They sagged in chairs together at the kitchen table, companions in fatigue and anxiety as they had not been in ease.

They were not modern. They could not view their daughter's elopement lightly. It might be said in the world at large that morals are not what they were, but the Parkers' morals were unmistakably what they were, and so were the morals, at least the professed morals, of the majority of the people in the town. Margaret's going off with a married man was to her parents a shocking thing and it was a thing that could mean nothing but unhappiness for her and shame for them. They minded. They minded terribly. Other people elsewhere, modern people, might make light of this sort of thing, but not the Parkers and not the town they lived in.

'If Cave's left his wife, she doesn't know it,' said Mr Parker, sitting at the table.

'Oh, George, you don't think he's – he's living with them both?' Flora could hardly utter the dreadful words.

'I don't know,' said George wearily. 'I don't know anything. That woman's genuinely expecting him home on Friday. I'll have to wait and see what I can find out then.'

They went to bed at last, but not to sleep. Flora had a very bad night, but she did not boast about it in the morning.

Thursday dawned and they rose to face it as best they could. James appeared expectantly, but was dashed to find he had been wrong.

'Well, you'll just have to wait and see if Cave's there tomorrow, though I wouldn't bet on it myself. You haven't had a paper this morning, I suppose, Mr Parker? I'm bringing some groceries in for Mrs Parker, so I'll bring some papers for you, shall I? News is bad. It looks as if it's war all right this time. It's not much good me studying to pass the College of Preceptors now, is it, Mr Parker? I shall have to join up, shan't I?'

His face gave him away. It betrayed the fact that he would rather face the enemy than the examination and Mr Parker smiled in sudden warmth and pity for his youth.

'We shall have to wait and see, James,' he said.

Left with the papers, Mr Parker had a bad morning. The general anxiety sharpened his own personal anxiety. Anxiety without, anxiety within, where was a man to turn? He felt as if a vast tide of war and trouble was rising and that he had to swim against it, to go in the opposite direction until he could recover something he had lost further back. When he had recovered it, then, and not until then, could he turn and go with the tide. Before the storm burst on the world, he must get Margaret safe, he must get her home.

He could not bear to be alone. He followed Flora about the house as she did her work. He helped her to make the bed and wiped the pots while she washed them. He was like an elderly child tagging about after its mother, and Flora fell back into the part of comforter as easily as if she had never laid it aside.

'Aren't you coming to sit down?' asked Mr Parker in the afternoon.

He himself was weary from lack of sleep by this time, but he could not settle without her. She came to sit with him in the drawing-room and they dozed uneasily in chairs.

It was towards the end of the afternoon that Mr Parker, receiving some message from his subconscious mind, opened his eyes and beheld Miss Fanny Martin coming up the back-garden path.

He clutched Flora, who woke with a start.

'Keep still,' he warned. 'Miss Fanny's in the back garden.'

Petrified, they stared.

'Can she see us?' whispered Flora.

'No, she can't,' George whispered back. 'But don't move, whatever you do.'

They watched.

'What does she want?' asked George wonderingly.

'Sheer curiosity,' said Flora. 'Front garden yesterday; back garden today.'

'She's coming up to the greenhouse.'

They flattened themselves still flatter against the back of their chairs.

'Oh dear,' quavered Flora.

'Keep still,' warned George. 'She won't see us if we don't move.'

Motionless, hardly breathing, they watched.

'Flora,' said George in a new tone. 'Look at her.'

'I'm looking,' said Flora grimly.

Miss Fanny's hat was bent in some search. She found what she wanted. She rose, unlocked the greenhouse door and stepped inside. The mouths of George and Flora at the back of the drawing-room fell open.

Miss Fanny stood in the greenhouse. Her face, under the lady-like straw hat, was lifted to the ripe tomatoes, but it was not the face of a lady at all. It was sly, greedy. As Miss Fanny put up her hands to his tomatoes, Mr Parker rose from his chair like a concertina expanding itself. Flora, with a smothered exclamation, pressed him into place again.

Miss Martin's predatory hands moved rapidly over the plants, twisting tomatoes from their stalks and putting them into the capacious pockets of her tweed coat. When she couldn't get any more into her pockets, she disposed tomatoes round her waist on both sides and buttoned the coat to keep them in place. There was no doubt that Miss Fanny was a very resourceful woman. Then she stepped outside, locked the door, replaced the key, and went down the path as she had come. The Parkers' eyes, in fascinated horror, were on her well-clad back, the waist-line, from the concealed tomatoes, not quite what it had been before.

As the door closed behind her, the spell broke. Mr Parker leapt to his feet, his eyes incredulous on Flora.

'Why, it's *her*!' he shouted.

'Yes,' said Flora. 'It's her all right.'

'She stole my tomatoes last year and she's stolen them again this!'

'Yes,' said Flora.

Mr Parker rushed to the greenhouse door, opened it and went in. He stood gazing at his denuded plants as if he couldn't believe what he had seen.

Flora followed him.

'Flora, if I hadn't seen it with my own eyes, I'd never have believed it,' he said solemnly. 'Never. It's dreadful. She could have afforded all the tomatoes she wanted. Why had she to come and steal these? Steal them. She's a thief.'

He gazed in bewilderment at Flora as if she could explain this astounding thing to him.

'Nay,' said Flora, shaking her head. 'I'm as thunderstruck as you are. I never liked her, but I never thought she'd do a thing like this. Coming and stealing our tomatoes? I'm absolutely flabbergasted. It isn't the actual tomatoes, you know, George,' said Flora sententiously. 'After all they don't *cost* much. It's what's behind it.'

'I know,' said George almost piteously. 'I can't get over it. Miss Fanny Martin!'

Deeply shocked, they were shocked together. Flora was shocked with George. She was too shocked to crow. She had no need to, either; Miss Fanny had done for herself as far as George was concerned; George would never hold Miss Fanny up as a model again.

'It's queer, isn't it, Flora?' said George, harping throughout the evening on what had happened. 'We went on in a rut for so long and now everything's changing. Everything's come at once, hasn't it? All in these two days?'

VII

If Flora needed further proof that George had swept Miss Fanny from her pedestal, she had it the next day when he led her out of the front door and down the main streets to the station.

'She daren't question us now,' he said. 'We don't need to keep out of her way; she'll take good care to keep out of ours.'

'But what about other people, George?' asked Flora.

A great deal, however, seemed to have been swept out with Miss Fanny, for George replied: 'Let them mind their own business.'

As it happened this new frame of mind was not put to the test, for again they met nobody.

Again they travelled to Westley, again the hills sank away behind them and the land flattened out to the sea.

'I doubt if he'll be there, George,' said Flora, goaded by suspense into saying something.

'We'll just have to wait and see,' said George, counselling a patience he was far from feeling himself.

'You wait here again, will you?' he said, planting Flora at the corner of Rosecroft Avenue. 'If he's there, there's going to be trouble and it's best you shouldn't be too near.'

'Oh, George,' said Flora. 'Don't get hurt.'

'Huh,' said George, stalking off like a bantam cock. 'It's not me who'll get hurt.'

At the gate of Mon Repos, his heart gave a great leap. Cave was actually there, bending over the new borders with his wife. At the creak of the gate, Mrs Cave turned.

'Oh, here's that funny little man again. I forgot to tell you he'd called.'

Cave turned then, and dropped the trowel.

'Go inside, Daisy,' he managed to get out.

Mr Parker strode across the borders regardless of damage to the seedlings.

'Come into the house, Cave,' he ordered, motioning towards it as if it were his own.

'Well, you stop here then, Daisy,' countermanded Cave, deadly white.

Mr Parker marched him into the front room and banged the door.

'Where is she?' he demanded.

Cave stood before him, a pitiable picture of a coward. His pale lips trembled, his long hands wavered uncertainly over his undulated hair, over his tie. He swallowed visibly and made an attempt to parry.

'Who?' he said.

'None of that,' said Mr Parker shortly. 'Where is she?'

'I don't know, Mr Parker. I don't really. I haven't seen her since Wednesday.'

'Wednesday? That's the day you took her from her home. What d'you mean, Wednesday?'

'I didn't *take* her, Mr Parker. She came of her own free will.'

'What d'you mean you haven't seen her since Wednesday?'

'I mean Wednesday, Mr Parker,' said the terrified Cave. 'I parted from her on Wednesday afternoon. We had a – a misunderstanding. It had all been a misunderstanding, Mr Parker, and she made the taxi drive to a Women's Hostel place in Ship Street in Trentham and that's all I know. Truly, Mr Parker, that's all I know, really.'

'You liar,' cried Mr Parker, leaping at him.

His impact took Cave unawares and sent him sprawling backwards into one of his newly-upholstered chairs, which, skidding across the room, brought down a table and a vase of cotton carnations. Before Cave could get up, Mr Parker was on him. He literally jumped on him, battering him with knees, feet and fists. Cave let him. He made no resistance. Mr Parker finally got his feet to the carpet again and stood glowering above the recumbent figure in the chair.

'Where is she?'

'I've told you the truth, Mr Parker,' wailed Cave. 'I've never seen her since Wednesday afternoon.'

'You liar. She left a letter saying she was going with you for ever and never coming home again. She'd burnt her boats. Why should she change her mind? She's not a girl to do that unless there's some good reason. What was it? Tell me what it was or I'll hit you again, you wretched cad, cringing there. Come on, out with it. She meant to go with you. Why didn't she?'

'Well . . .' began Cave, reluctantly.

'Go on,' ordered Mr Parker, prodding him.

'We *had* arranged to go together,' admitted Cave. 'But when it came to the point, I found I couldn't, Mr Parker. I couldn't leave my wife – not for good and all, I couldn't. Her health wouldn't stand it.'

'Oh,' said Mr Parker. 'You made your wife's health an excuse for not staying with her and then when it suited you, you made it an excuse for not leaving her? Eh?'

'We'd just bought this house,' quavered Cave in self-defence. 'We'd put all we'd got into it. I couldn't leave all this. I thought I could because I'm so fond of Margaret, but when it came to the point, duty won, Mr Parker.'

'Duty be damned,' said Mr Parker. 'I'd like to break every bone in your body. Messing about. Messing up other people's lives. You go and ruin the life of a good girl like Margaret and then you back out and leave her to face the music. You tried to enter into some hole-and-corner arrangement with her and she wouldn't have it. It was all or nothing for Margaret. She said it was all for love and the world well lost in her letter. But she found you weren't prepared to lose the world. Eh? I knew it. When she found you hadn't left your wife, she left you. Was that it?'

'Yes,' mumbled Cave.

'Where is she?' cried Mr Parker, making another violent assault.

He was hitting someone who daren't hit him back, but that did not deter him. On the contrary, he took the utmost advantage of it.

'Oh, Mr Parker, don't. Oh, don't . . .' besought Cave, from under his elbows. 'I tell you I left her at that hostel in Ship Street at Trentham. She may be there yet for all I know.'

'If I don't find her, I'll come back,' threatened Mr Parker, desisting, not from mercy, but from lack of breath. 'You can thank your stars I haven't broken every bone in your body. I would if I'd the time. But I'm going after my girl.'

He made for the door.

'You come poking your face into Sefton again and the police'll get you, so you know.'

'I'm not coming again, Mr Parker,' said Cave, not daring even to sit up, but remaining obediently where Mr Parker had thrust him. 'I've changed my district.'

'Well, I hold you in the hollow of my hand and don't you forget it. I might tell your firm at any time. And now you can call your wife in and tell her some more of your lies. Explain your black eye away as best you can. I've no doubt you'll do even that.'

Considerably disarranged in his own person, Mr Parker left the house.

Mrs Cave, after one look at him, gave a cry and rushed inside to see what had happened to her husband.

'George!' cried Flora in her turn. 'Has he hurt you?'

'Hurt me!' Mr Parker was contemptuous, straightening his tie. 'He daren't lift a finger against me, the coward. Margaret's never been with him. She wouldn't go with him, when she found he intended to live with them both. I did get that much out of him at any rate. He left her at a hostel in Ship Street at Trentham.'

'Is she still there?' cried Flora.

'We must go and see,' said George.

'Oh, poor girl, poor Margaret,' said Flora tearfully. 'She wouldn't dare to come home.'

'We must get there as quickly as possible. But I wish I hadn't

163

to keep hurrying you from place to place like this, Flora. It's too much for you.'

'It isn't George,' said Flora, hurrying with him.

'Well, take my arm, dear,' said George. 'And let me help you.'

VIII

More hurrying for trains, taxis, buses; more pushing past people, more swimming against the tide, fast rising now over the whole country and set strongly in one direction. Everybody everywhere was now talking to everybody else and on one subject: war. But the Parkers could take no part. Their agitation rising with the rising tide, they pushed against it to find Margaret.

They got to Trentham. They found the hostel. Directed to a bureau at the back of the hall, they put their question: Was Margaret Parker there?

'Yes,' said the young woman at the desk, referring to a book. 'She's here. But see, they're all just coming out of supper. You can find her for yourselves, can't you?'

A door had opened and a stream of girls and women poured into the hall and through it. The eyes of George and Flora, anxious, eager, tried to take stock of each face and form. The girls seemed to whirl past them; their eyes could not keep pace with them. Then they saw her, walking apart, her head down. Her face, before she saw them, was remote, desperate, and their hearts yearned over her.

Then she saw them and stood still. Her face went very

bright and happy for an instant, as if they were her salvation. Then she remembered why they were there and why she herself was there and she looked wildly to the entrance, to the refectory door behind, choosing her escape. But they reached her and took her hands. There was none of the righteous anger she had feared. It would have been hard for an observer to tell who was, or had been, in the wrong. For if she looked like an erring daughter, they looked no less like erring parents. There they stood, fearful in case forgiveness should be withheld, looking wistfully, Margaret at them and they at Margaret.

'Will you come home, love?' ventured Flora.

'We've come to fetch you,' said her father.

Margaret rolled her handkerchief into a ball in her hands. Her head was down again.

'I was trying to get a job,' she said.

'You can get a job from home,' said her father eagerly. 'You can come and help me at the shop if you like. James wants to join up, but even if he doesn't, you can come to the shop.'

'Come home, love,' urged Flora.

'Are you sure you want me?' asked Margaret in a low voice.

'We can't do without you,' said her father. 'We soon found that out.'

'I tried to do wrong,' said Margaret. 'It didn't come off, but I tried to go.'

'Nobody's ever going to say another word about that,' said Mr Parker. 'And nobody knows. So if you'll come home, it'll all be the same as before, only different,' he finished paradoxically.

'Go and get your case, love,' said Flora.'

'And now,' said Mr Parker, when, after midnight again, he closed the door of the house in Lawn Terrace behind them, 'we can face whatever's coming. If it's got to come, let it come. We can face it now. We're together.'

AFTER TEA

They had something to say to her, they told Christine. They would say it after tea.

Mr and Mrs Berry always fixed the time for everything. They arranged life in time-tables. Perhaps because nothing of importance happened to them, they liked to make unimportant things important. By fixing a walk, say, for three-thirty, the walk and the hour were made significant. One could look forward to three-thirty, refer frequently to three-thirty, get ready for three-thirty, announce that it was just three-thirty and with satisfaction set off. A walk, taken like that, was much more of an event than a mere exit from the garden gate as soon as a wish to walk occurred.

Mr Berry was a Civil Servant, but if anything of importance happened to him at his office, which was unlikely, he never said so.

While Mr Berry was at his office, Mrs Berry stayed at home, looking after herself. Mrs Berry was devoted to the care of herself and she expected the same devotion from Christine.

The neighbours were sorry for Christine.

'That poor girl,' they said to each other as Mrs Berry's voice fluted from the garden all the summer long.

'Christine, I'll have my orange juice now.'

'Bring my rug, Christine, I find it rather chilly.'

'Just get my sunshade from the corner of my wardrobe, Christine. Well if it's not there, it's somewhere else. Don't be stupid, dear.'

'They say an only child is spoilt,' said the neighbours to each other. 'But this one isn't. She can't call her soul her own.'

Mrs Berry arranged Christine's life in time-table too. Two mornings a week, she sent Christine into town to do the shopping. Mrs Berry did not care to go into town; it was too fatiguing. She did not care for people, either, and there were, unfortunately, so many of them. So she sent Christine to the shops. On the other mornings, she arranged what Christine should do to help Bertha, the maid, in the house.

In the afternoons, Christine took Mrs Berry for her walk. Mrs Berry leaned on Christine's arm and as she was a heavy woman and a great leaner, she almost sawed Christine's forearm in two.

'I think I'll come round to the other side now, Mother,' said Christine from time to time, letting the other forearm take its turn.

When mornings and afternoons were spent in this way, it seemed reasonable to Christine that she should have the evenings to herself. But in spite of a recent fierce struggle, she could not get them. She could not even get two evenings to attend the French lectures at the University.

'They're free,' she said, with tears of exasperation in her eyes. 'It's not as if I was asking you to pay anything for me.'

'Don't be impertinent, dear,' said Mrs Berry.

She explained that cost was not the point. The maid Bertha was already out two nights a week.

'But the lectures aren't on the same nights as Bertha's nights,' protested Christine.

'No, but if Bertha is out two nights a week and you are also out two nights a week, it makes everything very unsettled. Besides, your father likes you to be in when he comes home.'

'I don't know why,' sighed Christine. 'It's not as if we ever did anything.'

'I don't know what's come over you,' said Mrs Berry. 'You're getting very disagreeable.'

'Can I go to a lecture once a week then?' persisted Christine.

'I don't know,' said Mrs Berry. 'I shall have to see what your father says.'

So Christine waited with what patience she could. She was determined to improve her French somehow. She was determined to make up the deficiencies in her education of which, at nineteen, she was uncomfortably conscious. How could she keep pace with other girls if she didn't *know* anything, she asked herself furiously.

At school, her progress had been extremely hampered by Mrs Berry's headaches. Whenever Mrs Berry had a headache, she kept Christine at home. When Christine returned to school, she found she had lost her place in form. This happened so often that Christine, a clever child, lost heart and gradually relinquished her attempts to keep up. It was no good trying, she felt.

But lately she had been fired with a desire to know

something, to be something. Her friend Mary had gone off to London and was living a grand independent life with a flat of her own and a job of her own. When Mary wrote to ask Christine to join her, Christine tore the letter into tiny shreds so that no one should be able to piece together the preposterous, enchanting suggestion. If she could not even get permission to spend two nights a week at the French lectures, how could she hope to be allowed to go and spend her whole time in London? Mary and other girls might go off and pursue careers in London and elsewhere, but she had to stay at home.

She did, however, pursue a career of her own in secret. She entered for competitions in the literary journals. When she went into town to do the shopping, she rushed into the Public Library to see what she could go in for next.

The assistants there were quite familiar with the sight of the one they called 'the girl with the parcels'. Christine always had so many, because Mrs Berry did not believe in having things sent up. She believed in watching the cutting of the bacon, the weighing of the butter, and though she did not do this herself, she sent Christine to do it. And the bacon being cut and the butter being weighed, she believed in bringing them home there and then, in case the grocer, left to himself, should palm off some other bacon, some other butter.

So Christine, with parcels packed into the basket and dangling also from every finger, visited the reading room of the public library to go through the literary journals. She put down the basket and untwisted the string from her bleached fingers with relief. She collected the journals and sat down. She turned the pages with haste and excitement. Sometimes there was no mention of her, but sometimes 'Medea' had won a prize of two guineas, one guinea, or ten-and-sixpence for a set of verses, a short story or a limerick. After such an announcement, Christine collected her parcels and hurried from the library with flushed cheeks and shining eyes, and for days was down first in the morning to intercept the post-man. For these activities must be kept secret. She didn't know exactly why; but secret they must be kept.

'We all have our secrets,' she excused herself to herself.

Her mother, she knew, always had chocolates hidden in a corner of a drawer. She never brought them out to hand about. Her mother had chocolates hidden in a drawer and she, Christine, had nine pounds in notes hidden among the neat rolls of her mended stockings. It was the same thing. Human beings evidently were like that.

But although she knew about her mother's chocolates, had always known, she hoped her mother did not know about the nine pounds.

Perhaps it was that, she thought with sudden apprehension, perhaps it was the secreted money they were going to tell her about after tea.

Well, even if it was, she thought, she would have to wait. Nothing would induce them to disclose before the appointed time.

This habit of holding things back, of making them por-tentous, seemed to her most absurd. So many things about her parents seemed absurd, petty, tyrannical now. She didn't know when or how she had become critical and rebellious, but she was now both.

'I'm not treated half so well as Bertha,' she told them. 'I've no wages and I've no time off.'

It was this last outrageous remark that made Mr and Mrs Berry decide to tell her what they had intended to keep to themselves for another two years or even perhaps as long as they lived, letting it out only in their wills. But now they would tell her. They would bring her to her senses. Hers might be the accepted behaviour of the modern girl, but they would not put up with it. They would end it by explaining matters. They would tell her after tea.

At tea, Christine felt inclined to giggle. The atmosphere of the drawing-room was heavy with presage. Mr Berry, fair where he was not bald, small and solemn, sat on one side of the fire. Mrs Berry, fair and fuzzy, solemn but not small, sat on the other. Christine, slender, dark, glowing, and quite unlike either of them, sat between.

No one spoke. The clock ticked. The fire fell softly. When Mrs Berry drank tea, the resultant swallow sounded very loud. It made Christine more than ever inclined to giggle. She suppressed her smiles behind a biscuit. How could they hold things back like this? Why didn't they come out with it, whatever it was? Even if it was about the money, why didn't they come out with it?

'Will you have some more tea, James?' inquired Mrs Berry.

'Thank you, no,' said James.

'You may clear away, Christine,' said Mrs Berry.

Bertha was out.

Christine jumped up with alacrity. She seized the three-legged cake-stand and swung with it out of the room, endangering the Madeira. She came back for the tray and bore it out. She came back to fold up the table and the cloth.

Now for it. Now she would have to tell about her competitions and she didn't want to. She didn't want to at all. She wanted to keep something for herself.

'Close the door,' said Mrs Berry.

'Oh, must we have the door closed?' said Christine. 'It's hot in here and Bertha's out. She can't listen.'

'Close the door,' said Mrs Berry.

Yes, it was high time they told her. One could not even have the doors as one wanted them in one's own house without question these days.

'Your father and I have something to tell you, Christine,' said Mrs Berry when Christine was reseated. 'James, I think you'd better.'

James Berry gave a preliminary cough and pulled down his cuffs. He collected, as it were, Christine's attention. Although that was unnecessary because he already had it.

'I want you to prepare yourself for something of a shock, Christine,' he said.

Christine smiled. She was prepared, she thought, and it wouldn't be a shock.

'You are a sensible girl, on the whole,' conceded Mr Berry. 'And I think you will be able to stand it. We did not intend to tell you until you were twenty-one. If then.'

Mr Berry paused and Christine stared. This could not be about the money.

'We feel now that it would be better if you realised the exact position. You have been somewhat, shall we say, restive and undutiful lately,' said Mr Berry. 'You have upset your mother on several occasions. I say your mother, Christine, but there I come to the crux of the matter.'

Christine stared intently. What was coming? Something important this time. Something vital.

'She is not your mother, Christine,' said Mr Berry. 'Neither am I your father. We are not your parents and you are not our child. We took you from a Home when you were two years old. Your own parents were then dead.'

Christine sat quite still, staring at the man she had hitherto believed to be her father. The colour drained slowly from her cheeks.

'You must not take it too much to heart,' said Mr Berry. 'Everything shall be as before as far as we are concerned. We shall continue to do in the future what we have done for you in the past. But we think a little gratitude on your part would be more seemly. We think it is best that you should know what has been done for you.'

'Yes,' said Mrs Berry.

The colour was coming back now to Christine's cheeks. It deepened to a glow. Her eyes shone. Never had they seen such a lighting up of her face. This, they thought, was gratitude. Visible, satisfactory gratitude. How wise they had been to tell her.

They waited, for she was obviously going to speak when she could master her very proper emotion.

She leaned forward and they leaned forward, too, to accept.

'So you're not my parents after all?' she asked, rather breathlessly. 'I'm not your child? I'm no relation to you at all?'

'No,' they said.

'I can't take it in,' she said. 'I can't believe it.'

'It's true,' said Mrs Berry. 'I just walked through the Home and took the one with curly hair, didn't I, James?'

James signified gravely that this was so.

'You didn't legally adopt me? You didn't sign any papers?' asked Christine.

'No, there was nothing of that sort asked for seventeen years ago,' said Mr Berry.

'Besides, it meant settling money and so on,' said Mrs Berry. 'We didn't think it necessary. We always meant to treat you as our own daughter and we always have.'

'Then you are not bound to me in any way and I am not bound to you?' asked Christine.

'Only by such bonds as we have forged,' said Mr Berry sententiously. 'The bonds of affection.'

The light persisted in Christine's face.

'I ought to have guessed,' she murmured. 'Hiding those chocolates, for instance. No *mother* would do that. And this idea that you ought always to be getting something *out* of me. I felt it, you know – subconsciously. There were hundreds of indications. Why on earth couldn't I see?'

The faces of Mr and Mrs Berry were slowly and simultaneously assuming an expression of stupefaction, but she startled it away by throwing her arms up towards the ceiling and bursting into laughter.

They were alarmed. The shock had been too much for her. They had thought she was taking it so well, but it had made her hysterical.

'Christine,' said Mr Berry sternly. 'You must control yourself.'

'Yes,' said Mrs Berry.

Christine wiped her eyes.

'You're right. I must,' she said. 'But it's so marvellous.'

'Marvellous?' they inquired.

'Yes, marvellous. I'm not your child. You're not my parents. You adopted me for your own pleasure. I suppose you felt out of it because you had no children. I had curly hair. I was ornamental and you thought I'd be useful later. I have been useful. Useful and wretched. You've had quite as much out of me as I've had out of you. I thank you very much for what you've done, but I shan't stay.'

It was their turn to be struck dumb. They gaped.

'No, I shan't stay,' said Christine, getting up and still wiping her eyes. 'When nature provides parents one can't do anything but put up with them. But I can. You chose me when I had no voice in the matter, but now I have and I don't choose you. You are not at all the sort of parents I should choose. By the way, do you happen to know my name?'

They were still too dumfounded to speak.

'My name?' said Christine. 'I should like to know my name, please.'

'Your name,' spluttered Mr Berry suddenly finding his voice. 'Is Higgins.'

'Oh,' said Christine. 'Well, it's mine, anyway. Now, don't take this too much to heart. You'll probably get someone to do for you what I have done, but I'm afraid you'll have to pay her. I shall go to Mary for the present. I have enough money to keep me until I get a job. I made it in competitions, you know. I shall go into service if all else fails. I've always envied Bertha.'

She made for the door.

'You're not going *now?*' cried Mrs Berry.

'Yes, I'm going now,' said Christine. 'I'll return these clothes to you as soon as I can get others. Goodbye and thank you so very much for telling me.'

'James!' cried Mrs Berry.

But what could James do?

WEDNESDAY

Mrs Bulford, as she still called herself, kept passing and re-passing the double wooden doors, standing wide open to make a gap in the garden wall. Every time she passed she glanced in at the house. She did no more than glance, but with every glance she saw a little more. She saw something else; a hoop lying on the lawn; Elsie as she stood at the kitchen window examining her nails in the pause between the courses in the dining-room. Mrs Bulford, Elsie's former mistress, knew how particular Elsie was about her nails, how she brooded over every little break or blemish, blaming her work, threatening to leave, insisting on the best soap if ever she had to wash anything.

Passing again, Mrs Bulford saw Elsie going past the passage window with a tray. She must be taking the pudding in now. Perhaps it was the children's favourite: Queen's Pudding with meringue on the top. Pat used to bang his spoon on the table with joy when this pudding came in; but probably he was too old for that now. Mrs Bulford hoped it wasn't Queen's Pudding today because the children ate it so slowly, making it last. They wouldn't hurry, she feared, even though they knew their mother was waiting outside the gate.

Preoccupied with the innocent cruelty of her children, Mrs Bulford walked quite a long way beyond the house before she turned back. The trees hung over the garden walls, making a pleasant irregular shade. There were the familiar drowsy summer sounds; the doves cooing from the Watsons' roof, the faint sound of someone's wireless, far away from the hum of the city.

The road was empty. The families living in the pleasant houses were all within, having lunch. Parents and children sitting round the table, the subdued clatter of spoons and forks, intimate small talk. 'Don't spill, darling.' 'I got all my sums right this morning, Mummy.' 'I saw Mrs Parsons in town. I haven't seen her for ages.' 'Please may I have some more?'

Mrs Bulford laid her hand on the wall as she walked. Behind this it was all going on as before. She alone was shut out. She was shut out of the house, waiting for her children to finish their pudding at a table presided over by Cecil's new wife. Another woman sat in her place, did her hair at her dressing-table, slept in her bed, bought clothes for her children.

She was shut out of the town too, because she shrank from being seen in it. She had taken rooms in a village on the out-skirts, just far enough away not to be known, she had fancied. But by this time, everyone in the village knew all about her; she saw it in their eyes.

Half the time, she couldn't believe that such a thing had happened to her. She would lie in bed, her arms behind her head, looking round at the cottage bedroom, at the pink-washed walls, the yellow furniture with white china knobs on the drawers, and think 'It can't be. How have I got here?'

She had the wholly unwarranted feeling that she might be able to go home sometime. She was like an exile waiting all the time to go home, devouring news of the place she longed to be in. She bought the Beddingworth papers, morning and evening, and read every word, even the advertisements. She knew who was born and who died or was married, she knew who wanted domestic help or houses. Every train that passed through to Beddingworth, she felt she ought to be on it. If anyone so much as mentioned the name of the city, a pang went through her. Though when she lived there, she had taken little interest. She had other things to do, she had so much . . . Now she had nothing. She did nothing but wait for the first Wednesday of the month; the first Wednesday, fixed by Cecil's lawyers as the day when she, not a fit and proper person to have custody of her children, could, as a concession on Cecil's part, nevertheless see them for a few hours in the afternoon.

The children were quite used to these Wednesdays now, that was why they didn't hurry out. After all, it had been going on for almost eighteen months. The separation had grown less painful for them; more painful for her. But it was better that way. Anything was better than that first terrible Wednesday when they hadn't been able to understand, at the end of the afternoon, why she couldn't go back into the house with them. They had tried to pull her inside the gate, crying: 'Why don't you come in, Mummy? You must come in. Don't go away again. Don't go, Mummy. Come in . . .' She had seen the alarmed faces of Elsie, the daily woman, and Cecil's new wife at the windows. Then Elsie came out to get the children in, and she had to tear her skirt from their hands and go away, weeping. She could hear them calling after her as she went.

She thought she could never face another Wednesday after that. It would be better to go right away, never try to see them again, she decided. But on the first Wednesday of the next month, she could not help herself. She was at the gates, walking up and down, waiting for them as she waited now.

Passing the house again, she saw that the nursery windows were thrown wide; she was glad of that. She saw there were new curtains at her bedroom windows. Perhaps everything was new there now. When she had come to sort out the things that were hers, to take away, they made such a pitiful collection that she had left them. Keep them, keep them, she had cried to Cecil. He had kept them and presumably his new wife had them now.

He had married the very week the decree was pronounced absolute, and she didn't know who his wife was. That was what was so extraordinary; she didn't know where he had got her from. During her life with Cecil, she had never heard of anybody called Sheila. Yet he must have known her all the time he was getting the divorce. He had always been secretive. He had always known how to hide things, even the most trivial, and she herself never had, or she would not have been walking up and down outside the wall now.

He must have been watching all the time. He must have seen the affair with Jack dawning, developing and giving him his opportunity. He edged her into adultery, set the trap and watched her fall into it. He could not afford misconduct himself; he was a lawyer and his practice would have been ruined. Her idiotic infatuation for Jack was the chance he must almost have despaired of, because she had never given way to, or even felt, such a temptation before.

It had all been very short-lived. It was over in three days. She had pretended to go to Aunt Julia's, had gone to London with Jack instead, and after three days, the private detective got them.

It had been a temporary madness, induced by loneliness, the cold withdrawal of Cecil, the approach of middle-age. She felt her looks were going, she made a last grab at the romance she had missed. She felt that if she didn't get it then, she would have missed it for ever, and how sad to die without having loved or been loved. As it stood on the horizon like the sun about to go down into night, love seemed the most important thing in life and Jack, to her almost incredulous happiness, seemed to love her as Cecil had never done.

He was good-looking, several years younger than she was, weak and frightened of life. She felt she made him strong by her love, but it had all been an illusion. When they were found out, his horrified family came and bore him away to safety; the safety of not having to marry her. As if she would ever have married him! She was deeply hurt that he should have thought she would try to make him marry her.

Anyway, he had gone abroad. The suit was undefended. The whole affair rebounded to her shame and hers alone. It was all heaped on her and she accepted it. She was so overwhelmed by it that she never looked up to see what Cecil was doing. She accepted the proceedings as her due; she told herself that she deserved the worst and made no protest.

For several months she felt this. But afterwards she had seen more clearly. She saw that Cecil had calculated everything; and sometimes as she brooded in the cottage bedroom, she felt that if there was fairness anywhere, not in this world, but in what she vaguely thought of as 'afterwards', she felt he would be faced with a meaner sin than hers.

As she reached the gates again, she saw the children passing the staircase window, going up to put on their outdoor things. Cecil and his wife were standing together in the garden, admiring the sweet peas. She saw the sun shining on the girl's fair hair. She was young.

The whole thing was oriental really, thought Mrs Bulford. Ageing wife got rid of, young one put in her place. But since nature discriminates against women, why should men do otherwise?

When she found herself on the verge of middle-age, she should have dug herself in, she thought grimly, and kept her children, kept her place in the house and in the world. Instead, she had gone gallivanting after Jack and lost everything. What a spectacle she had made of herself! What an ugly, exposed thing to do! It was like one of those bad dreams where you find yourself in a public place with nothing on but your vest. Only from this dream there was no waking.

She was still walking in the opposite direction when the children came out of the gate, Pat, aged six, examining with absorbed interest a toy aeroplane in his hand. She turned and saw them and came hurrying, a stout figure in a tight coat and skirt; in spite of her suffering, she grew steadily fatter.

'Darlings,' she said breathlessly. What happiness to kiss their round, smooth cheeks. They let her, and she kissed them over and over again, greedily, until Pat drew off, frowning a little, and gave his attention to his plane again.

'Mumsie's going to buy me a Comet when she goes out this afternoon,' he announced. 'Is she, darling?' said Mrs Bulford brightly. 'How nice of her.'

That was how it had been arranged. She was 'Mummy' and her supplanter was 'Mumsie'. The children had jibbed at it at first. They wouldn't say it. But they said it now without a thought, she could see.

Mrs Bulford took Susan's hand and drew Catherine's arm through hers. She blinked back the tears of happiness and emotion that had come into her eyes, and saw Susan looking up at her with curiosity. Nine-year-old Susan wondered why anybody grown-up should cry. Surely when you were grown-up and could do as you liked, you had no need to cry?

Mrs Bulford squeezed Catherine's arm against her side and smiled lovingly at her tall daughter. Catherine smiled in a constrained way and looked across the road. She let her arm lie in her mother's for several minutes. Then she withdrew it. Mrs Bulford went on smiling and pretended not to notice. But a pang went through her. Perhaps somebody had said something. Catherine was thirteen, she was beginning to know what her mother had done. She was beginning to judge her with the ignorance and intolerance of the young.

'Now what would you like to do this afternoon?' asked Mrs Bulford brightly. 'Where would you like to go?'

'The Little Park,' said Pat. 'I want to fly my plane on the grass so if it makes a crash landing it won't matter.'

'Would you like to do that, girls?' asked Mrs Bulford.

They nodded.

'We'll go to the Little Park then,' said Mrs Bulford. 'But wait a moment, Susan, let me do your hair again.'

No one could do Susan's hair but her. The child had looked a sight ever since she left her. She took a pocket comb from her bag and the little group halted on the pavement while she combed out Susan's thick fair hair. That woman would never learn that Susan's hair should be tied securely almost on the crown of her head. She would let the bow dangle heavily over the child's ear, ruining the effect.

'There you are, darling,' said Mrs Bulford, passing her hand over Susan's head like a blessing.

They walked on, Mrs Bulford in the midst of them. For the next few hours they were hers.

'Now tell me all you've been doing since last month,' she said, drawing Catherine's arm within hers again. It might have been her fancy that Catherine withdrew it last time. Perhaps there was nothing wrong really. She knew how apt she was to look for slights and coldness now.

Catherine, her arm lying inertly along her mother's, shrugged her shoulders and said she didn't think she'd been doing anything. Pat was too absorbed to answer. What did he care about last month when he had this plane in his hand today? Susan remembered she had lost a tooth and showed her mother the gap.

'Oh, did it hurt?' asked Mrs Bulford with concern.

'No. Mumsie pulled it out. I only felt a little tweak. Mumsie gave me sixpence for being brave.'

Mrs Bulford felt a sharp pang of jealousy, which she tried to suppress. She knew she ought to feel glad that Cecil's new wife was kind to her children. And it wasn't the girl's fault that Cecil had married her. If it hadn't been her, it would have been someone else. Mrs Bulford told herself these things; but remained jealous.

Catherine, murmuring that there was something wrong with her belt, removed her arm from her mother's, fiddled with her waist and did not replace the arm.

'So there is something wrong,' thought Mrs Bulford.

They reached the Little Park, a bright, new, open place with an artificial stream running over a cement bed, looped by hump-backed cement bridges. On the cement shores of a shallow lake, blue, red, green and yellow boats were drawn up. Everything was miniature, Walt Disneyish, except that in a caged enclosure sat one solitary monkey quite out of key, forlorn, flea-bitten and, in spite of the heat, shivering. The children were always sorry for this monkey. Catherine held out her hand and murmured tenderly.

She has pity for the monkey, thought Mrs Bulford, but not for me.

If I'd been an animal, she thought, people would have been kinder.

The children asked for money to buy nuts. The monkey received one or two with a listless air and dropped them to the floor of the cage. Susan looked as if she might cry, so Mrs Bulford suggested they should go in the boats. The two younger children seized more money and ran off. Catherine didn't want to go in a boat, but when she realised that she would otherwise be left alone with her mother, she hastily said she would take one too.

The boats, safe, flat-bottomed affairs, were only for children; sixpence each for half-an-hour. So Mrs Bulford waited half-an-hour, watching Pat and Susan enjoy themselves, and Catherine drift moodily on the water. She sat on a hard little bench in the sunshine, surrounded by stiff bright flowers in the flowerbeds.

When the half-hour was up, the children clamoured to ride on the miniature railway. They were with one who would give them anything they asked, so they took every advantage of it. Mrs Bulford packed her stout form in with them and rode round the Park bulging over the side of the little wooden wagon.

When that was over, they wanted ice-cream. They bought little tubs with cardboard spoons and sat on a bench with their mother, scooping out very small tastes of ice-cream to make it last. Even Catherine was a child again, thus engaged. When they had finished the ices, they sat looking about them for further opportunity for pleasure.

'Susan, how is that toe of yours?' asked Mrs Bulford. 'Is it better?'

'It hurts sometimes,' said Susan.

'Take off your shoe and sock, darling, and let Mummy see,' said Mrs Bulford.

'Oh, you can't,' said Catherine. 'Not here, what will people think?'

'You mustn't mind so much what people think,' said her mother.

'I think it's better to,' said Catherine in a low voice, turning her head away.

Mrs Bulford took Susan's soft little foot into her hand. The feel of it moved her unbearably. What a loss – not to be able to touch her children every day, any time of night or day as she used to, not to know their limbs, their bodies any more. Once she had known them better than her own. She closed her fingers over Susan's foot and could hardly see it for a moment.

But she repressed her tears. She knew how mystified and oppressed the children were by signs of adult grief. She spread Susan's toes out, soothing the small pink mark that showed on one.

'You must always be very careful about your shoes, Susan,' she said. 'You must ask – Mumsie – to see that this toe has plenty of room. You have feet like mine, the third toe is as long as the second. So many shoes don't allow for that.'

'D'you remember how we used to play "This little pig went to market" when we came into your bed in the mornings?' asked Susan, laughing up into her face. She said it without any sadness; she said it as if all that wasn't over, but could be resumed at any time.

'Yes, I remember,' said Mrs Bulford. 'Now, let's put your sock on again. I think it must be time for tea.'

'Hurray,' said Pat, sliding off the bench at once. 'I'm hungry.'

Tea was the crown of the afternoon, not only for the children but for Mrs Bulford. Sitting like any other mother with her children at the table, pouring out tea for them, spreading Pat's bread-and-butter with jam, wiping his fingers, entering into indulgent co-operation with the waitress to give them all they wanted, Mrs Bulford almost had the illusion that she had never left them.

Pat, his aeroplane out of sight and mind under his chair, was able to give his mother his attention. He was getting what he wanted, she was giving him things. She was letting him have another cream bun, so, his chin only an inch or two above his plate, he beamed on her.

'You *are* kind, Mummy,' he said with sudden fervour. Then added, as if to explain this to himself: 'But I are a little bit your boy, aren't I?'

Mrs Bulford put the tea-pot down on the provided tile with a slight crash.

Susan was disgusted with her brother.

'Of course you're Mummy's boy. She *borned* you,' she said. 'She doesn't live with us now, but she's still our Mummy, aren't you, Mummy? Can I have another cream bun, too?'

Mrs Bulford passed the plate of buns with a smile. They couldn't help it. They didn't understand. She didn't know which hurt most, Pat's confusion, Susan's matter-of-fact acceptance, or Catherine's judgment.

Everything seemed to have a barb in it today. But probably every Wednesday would be worse than the one before. The children would grow further and further away from her. They would become used to 'Mumsie', to the situation, they would come to look upon her as a nuisance, their own affairs would absorb them increasingly. So long as she could provide entertainment they would come happily with her perhaps, but when they could find entertainment for themselves, would they want her?

She paid the bill. It came to quite a lot. But that didn't matter; she had three weeks to save in for the next Wednesday. It was perhaps as well that she was not allowed to see the children oftener; she couldn't afford to.

'Are we going home now?' asked Pat eagerly. 'P'raps my Comet is there now. P'raps it's waiting. I think Mumsie will be back now.'

'Yes, you're going back now,' said his mother.

Heartless little boy, she thought. But why blame him for the mess she had made of her life? What had a child of six to do with the emotional tangles of a middle-aged woman?

The little party returned along the leafy road, Mrs Bulford setting a slow pace to keep them with her as long as possible.

Then, turning the corner, walking towards them arm in arm, came Cecil and his new wife.

Mrs Bulford, her eyes fixed upon them, came to a standstill. She could not face such an encounter. But Pat, breaking away from his mother, ran towards them shouting: 'Mumsie! Did you get it? Did you get it, Mumsie?'

Susan raised her eyes to her mother. 'May I go too?' she asked.

'Certainly, darling. But kiss Mummy goodbye first,' said Mrs Bulford.

Catherine stood awkwardly with her mother.

'You'd better go too, dear,' said Mrs Bulford. She kissed

the girl's smooth brow. 'Goodbye. I'll see you on the fourth, won't I ?'

Catherine nodded.

'Goodbye,' she said.

The group had reached the gate. Cecil raised his hat to the woman he had lived with for fifteen years. Pat disappeared with his parcel; Susan waved vigorously, Catherine with restraint. Then they were gone.

Mrs Bulford turned and walked back the way she had come. She could not bring herself to pass the house yet.

But later when the dusk was deeper, she passed it on her way to the bus. Elsie had just come out to pick up the hoop on the lawn. Upstairs someone was drawing the curtains, first at one window, then at another. They were all gathered in for the night. Everything was very quiet. Even from the gate she could smell the sweet peas. She walked away down the road.

SUMMER HOLIDAY

We were overjoyed to hear that Rose was going with us to the sea. Rose was the nicest nurse-maid we had ever had. She was young and pretty and romped with us. Everybody loved her. My mother was indulgent with her. She did for Rose what she had never done for any other nurse-maid; she let her have her young man for tea on Sundays.

His name was Frank. He was long and lanky, with big hands and feet. He was quiet and kind. On Saturdays and Sundays he came with Rose when she took us out, and we hardly ever let them have any peace. We swung on their hands. We made them run. We dodged and played round the pair of them and altogether took up all their attention. But I don't think they minded. They were at the beginning of love and were shy with each other. Perhaps it was a relief to be together and yet with a pack of children who allowed no embarrassed silences.

We didn't as a rule take to visitors in the nursery, but we accepted Frank's large, peaceable presence as a matter of course. Rose sat at one end of the table and Frank at the other. The twins, Roger and Charles, were on one side, and I and my sister, Ellie, on the other. Ellie would never let me sit next to Frank. I was eight and she was only six, but she always got her own way.

'I love Frank,' she would say, taking her spoon out of her mouth to beam at him, and he would blush and laugh and avoid Rose's eyes.

'I love Frank,' Ellie announced once. 'And when I grow up, I'm going to marry him.'

'You can't, silly,' said Roger, who at ten was very superior. 'He's going to marry Rose.'

At this both Rose and Frank went crimson. Then they smiled happily and shyly at each other as if something was now openly acknowledged between them.

Rose was as excited as we were about going to the sea, although she didn't know what she was going to. She had never seen the sea. We couldn't get over that.

'Never seen the sea?' we kept saying, sibilant with an unwaning astonishment. *'Never seen the sea?'*

Frank had. He had been to Blackpool.

'Some day you and me'll go to the sea together, won't we, Rose?' he managed to get out at tea that last Sunday.

You never knew what my sister Ellie would do or say next. Something now moved her to get down from her chair and throw her arms round Frank.

'Don't leave, Frank,' she said appealing to us as if we had anything to do with it. 'Let him come too.'

'It's not a case of being let, love,' said Rose. 'It's a case of not being able to get, isn't it, Frank? Frank couldn't leave his work. He couldn't get off.'

'Couldn't you?' said Ellie, looking searchingly into his face.

'Oh, no,' said Frank. 'Unheard of, me getting off at this time of the year.'

He smiled and smoothed her curls back with a big, careful hand.

'I'll send you a postcard,' I said, wanting to get in somewhere, if Ellie would let me. 'That is, it depends if I can.'

I meant if I had the money. I knew how soon our pennies disappeared at the sea, but I intended to spare enough for a postcard for Frank if I possibly could.

We clung to Frank until the last minute. I don't think we let him have a word alone with Rose. When he was going he managed to take her hand and say: 'Don't forget me, Rosie, will you?' She shook her head and smiled up at him. She stood at the door a long time watching him until he was out of sight.

The next morning we were off, wild with excitement. We hadn't been to Port St John before, and the long train journey was full of conjecture as to what it would be like, and if the landlady of Bay View whose name, we had been told, was Mrs Simpson, would let us take our buckets full of sea-water and crabs upstairs or would she make us leave them in the porch, where goodness knew what would happen to them.

'Where do you get crabs from?' asked Rose in mystification.

'From the shore,' we told her.

'Are they walking about?' asked Rose, as if she didn't like the idea.

We realised that she had only seen the sort of crab there is at the fishmonger's.

'Oh, they're not like that,' we cried. 'See,' said one of the boys, taking up Ellie's hand and showing Rose the nail on her little finger. 'They're smaller even than that.'

'Well, I never,' breathed Rose.

When we had eaten everything we had brought with us and made Rose tell all the stories of her childhood she could remember, we began to sag a little. Ellie went to sleep. I got pins and needles in my dangling legs. The boys kept sighing. Our parents travelled in the next compartment. In those days fathers were not disturbed.

At last, we left the train, such an excitement to get into and such a relief to get out of, and the sea air blowing down the platform revived us at once. We piled into an open carriage, with Rose on the box beside the coachman and all the luggage to come on by out-porter. We bowled down a side-street and suddenly the little scene of Port St John burst upon us.

'The sea, Rose! The sea!' we shouted, and she turned round with one speechless smile and turned back again.

Below her in the well of the carriage, incommoding our parents and endangering ourselves, we struggled to see everything at once; the little bay, the smooth sands, the grass-topped cliffs, the crescent of tall white houses on the little promenade. The carriage drew up at one of these, with Bay View painted on the gate-post, and Mrs Simpson appeared as if by magic to welcome us. We saw at once that she was kind and that there would be no restrictions.

We trooped upstairs after her to the first-floor front sitting-room which was to be ours. In a body we rushed to the bay window to make sure we could see the sea. It was all right; we could see all of it. We hung out of the windows, ecstatically surveying the scene of our holiday, until we were taken away to our bedrooms.

Here Ellie and I were luckier than anybody else, because we

could see the sea again from the room, over our sitting-room, where we were to sleep with Rose. There was a big bed near the window for Ellie and me, and a small bed against the wall by the door for Rose. We shut ourselves in here with Rose and whispered gleefully while we washed our hands and faces, because the boys couldn't see the sea from their windows and were protesting that it wasn't fair.

Looking back, all the summers of childhood seem to have been fine and warm, but this one was really so. Day after day, the sun shone, the sea sparkled, the sand was warm to our bare feet. Ellie and I didn't see much of our brothers. They had entered into what they called an Adventure League, which took them far afield and kept them busy. Our parents knew nothing of the League, which was perhaps as well, but the twins sometimes boasted to us about hanging head downwards over the cliff, or jumping a chasm. Truly feminine even at our tender age, we thought they were wonderful, but had no wish to do likewise.

We were supremely happy with Rose. Rose was the perfect companion, as good to play with as a child, yet affording the security only a grown-up can give to children. Rose did everything with us except bathe. She wouldn't bathe, but she paddled, holding up her print skirts and bending into the sea to exclaim at all she saw.

'A bubble keeps coming up in the sand here,' she would call out. 'What does that mean?'

'Cockles. Or crabs,' we told her importantly. It was something deliciously new for us to be able to tell anybody anything.

'Oh! a lot of tiny little silver fish,' she cried. 'Just as if somebody'd spilled a packet of pins in the water.'

Her comparisons were always homely. The little round jellyfish stranded on the shore reminded her of the cut-glass butter dishes at home, the ones with the pattern in the middle.

Sometimes we played in a little thicket behind Bay View because of the wild convolvulus there. It seemed incredible to Ellie and me that no one should want these trumpet-flowers of purest white but us. You had only to pluck a trail and it made the most beautiful crown of stem and leaf and flower. We made crowns for ourselves and Rose. She looked lovely in hers. We made her sit on a bank and be the queen, and we curtsied and sang to her and she bore it with tireless good humour.

Just as we never lost sight of the sea on this holiday, we never lost sight of Rose either. She was with us all day and all night too. When we woke in the morning, there she was in her bed across the room. It was very satisfactory. We felt complete; nothing was missing. Rose gave you this feeling; as if, when she was there, everything was all right.

Bay View was a big house and there were other families staying in it, but since there were no children of our ages among them, we didn't take any notice of them. Until one day two young men arrived to occupy the smallest sitting-room, which was over the front door and next to ours. In the morning it had been empty. When we came in to lunch, the door was open and the two young men were standing in the room. One was pink and fair and spent his whole time on the shore, trying to get sunburnt with such success that his face went scarlet, swelled, swelled and finally peeled. We never knew what his name was.

But the other young man, Rose soon told us, was called Mr Salter. He had dark wavy hair and my mother said he was flashy. We thought she meant because his eyes and teeth flashed in the dimness of the landing, as they certainly did when we passed him with Rose several times a day. Mother said she didn't like his shoes. Ellie and I looked at them next time we met him. They were white, criss-crossed with brown straps. We couldn't see why mother objected to them; neither could Rose.

We came across Mr Salter all the time. Not only had he the little sitting-room next to ours, but he slept on the second floor where we slept. Mr Salter began by trying to make friends with Ellie and me. He tweaked our hair and said we were 'nice kids'. But we weren't taken in. We knew he wasn't interested in us. It was Rose he wanted to get to know.

Rose had been pretty before, but she was prettier than ever now. She was so happy to be out in the sun all day with us. She glowed. With her sun-flushed cheeks, her laughing blue eyes and her rumpled curly hair, she seemed prettier by far than anybody in Port St John. Mr Salter evidently thought so too.

'Good morning, beauty,' I heard him say to her on the stairs.

'Now, Rose,' said my mother warningly once or twice.

'Oh, there's no harm, 'm!' said Rose, laughing and blushing.

In those days, there was no pier, no bandstand at Port

St John, there were no trippers, no concert parties. But the year we were there, it was decided to hold a carnival. My father was displeased, and he said he hadn't come for that sort of thing, but we were delighted, although we were told that nothing of it would happen until we were in bed.

With absorbed interest we watched the fairy lights being looped up along the promenade. They looked particularly dead as they hung there, but Rose said they would be lovely on Carnival night and we waited almost breathlessly for that.

Rose asked for the evening off. I think my mother must have been guarding her for Frank, because she was reluctant about the evening. But I suppose she couldn't very well refuse and Rose got her permission.

We entered whole-heartedly into Rose's preparation for the Carnival. She washed her hair. She pressed her best white dress in Mrs Simpson's kitchen while we looked on. We went with her to buy confetti to throw at people, but when we got to the shop we persuaded her to buy paper rose petals instead because they were prettier. Coming away, we were as doubtful as she was as to whether she had done the right thing. Rose petals were more for weddings, she said. She bit her lower lip and said she doubted whether she'd dare throw them at anybody. She cheered up when I said she could throw them at Mr Salter, though privately I considered it a pity to waste rose petals on him.

The day of the carnival arrived, and seemed long to us. Everybody was waiting for the evening, and when the dusk at last began to fall, it seemed strangely significant. The sky over the sea changed from primrose to pearly grey. The sea lapped the shore with small crystal waves, and because we were watching for the dark as we had never watched before, we saw for the first time how beautiful everything was.

Rose put us to bed as usual, but it was understood that we should get up again as soon as she had gone. Not until, she said, because she was late. From our pillows we watched her getting ready, which she did with amazing speed; washing with her pink scented soap, brushing her hair furiously, getting into her white dress, doing her hair all over again, and all the time breathing fast and smiling with excitement.

'Now, goodbye,' she said, snatching her bag of rose petals and kissing us.

'Be good, won't you.'

As soon as the door closed, we got out of bed and posted ourselves at the window, our bare feet on Mrs Simpson's cold linoleum. And suddenly all the lights went on and we cried out in delight. They bloomed like flowers garlanding the bay; and over the sea the stars came out. It was magic and unforgettable. A band struck up somewhere and the people thronging the promenade laughed louder and moved faster, and showers of confetti began to spurt out everywhere. From our windows we quite plainly made out Rose in her white dress. She was emptying her bag of rose petals over Mr Salter and when she had done it, she ran away and Mr Salter ran after her, pelting her with confetti. We laughed with pleasure to think what fun she was having. For quite a long time we saw her white dress running like a ribbon through the crowd. Then she was lost to view.

It grew darker and though the lights waxed brighter and the Carnival gayer, our feet were colder and colder. We were driven into bed in the end to warm them, and in warming them, we fell asleep.

I woke suddenly. I felt someone strange was in the room. The moon was high and pouring its light through the open window. Cautiously, I craned over the top of the sheet. A man was kneeling on the floor by Rose's bed. I knew it was Mr Salter by his shoes.

I turned over with relief and was falling asleep again when Ellie woke. She was going to sit up, but I pulled her down under the clothes.

'It's only Mr Salter,' I whispered into her ear and we giggled, until Ellie suddenly said in a loud voice:

'I've lost my shell.'

She always took a shell to bed with her; it was only half a cockle shell, but she liked it.

We came up out of the middle of the bed and heard Rose's voice asking sharply: 'What's the matter over there? What are you two doing?'

We sat up in bed. There was no one there but Rose. Mr Salter had gone.

'Ellie's lost her shell,' I said.

'Gracious, is that all?' said Rose. 'Lie down, both of you. We'll find it in the morning.'

On other nights after that, we woke briefly, knew Mr Salter was there and fell asleep again. Children are incalculable beings. I don't know why we didn't say anything about it, then, either to Rose or to our parents. Except that it wasn't important to us. No more important than, and no different from, meeting Mr Salter on the stairs.

But, although we didn't entirely grasp it, he spoilt this middle part of our holiday. He was always in the offing. If we made sandcastles on the shore, he was somewhere about, throwing pebbles at Rose or calling out to her and generally taking her attention from us. Rose wasn't ours any more. She was restless, she was even, I sometimes felt, a bit silly.

One afternoon, Mr Salter tracked us down to our special secret place, the thicket at the back of Bay View. We had just made a convolvulus crown for Rose and were fitting it to her head, when there he was, standing with his feet wide apart, jingling money in his trouser pockets and staring at Rose with a queer sort of smile.

'Hop it, you two,' he said to us, but still staring at Rose.

'No, they mustn't,' said Rose quickly. 'They can't.'

'But they can,' he said and taking sixpence from his pocket he held it out. 'Go and spend that, the pair of you,' he said. 'And don't hurry back.'

We took the sixpence. We didn't want to stay in the thicket with him there. We ran off to the shops. It was an adventure to be out alone and we enjoyed it.

In some undefined way, Mr Salter made me remember Frank, if only to say to myself that he wasn't half so nice. When I had bought an ice-cream for each of us, I spent the rest of the sixpence on a postcard for Frank. It was a picture of the crescent and Ellie and I were finding Bay View on it, when Rose came up, looking worried.

'You've been a long time,' she said.

'Look, we've bought this postcard for Frank,' I said, showing her.

She didn't look at it. She turned away her head and bit her lip. We felt quite anxious as we went in for tea, but not for long. Grown-ups were always strange beings to us, even Rose, and it was no good trying to understand them.

After tea I wrote on the postcard and took it to Rose.

'Will you write the address?' I asked her.

She turned a strange look upon me.

'What have you put on that card?' she said.

'Love and kisses,' I said, 'isn't that right?'

She made a queer sort of laugh and took my pencil to write Frank's address.

The next morning, after breakfast, Ellie and I were amazed to see Mr Salter and his friend leaving Bay View with their suitcases. Their holiday was over. We craned out of the window to watch them go, but Rose wouldn't watch. She kept to the back of the room.

The nuisance of Mr Salter was ended. Ellie and I were delighted. Rose was ours again. She was quieter, not so gay as she had been, but she was kinder than ever to us, as if she wanted to make up for something, and our last days at Port St John were filled with happiness to the brim.

We travelled home on Saturday, because my father wanted to be in his office on Monday morning. We left the sea with great regret, but as soon as our faces were turned towards home, we were glad to be going back.

'Will Frank come to tea tomorrow?' we asked Rose.

'I think so,' she said, in what we felt was a queer way.

'Aren't you sure?' we said.

'Oh! Yes, I'm sure he'll come,' said Rose more normally.

The next afternoon, when we heard his big feet crunching the gravel on the path round the side of the house, we rushed in a body to meet him. We were delighted to see him. He looked nicer than ever. We pushed and pulled at him like Lilliputians at a Gulliver and dragged him up to the nursery where Rose was setting the table for tea.

She went very red when she saw him and didn't seem to be able to say even 'Hello!'

But Frank wasn't so shy as he had been and said:

'You look fine, Rose. You're brown. Did you enjoy yourself?'

'Oh, yes,' said Rose, putting the cake on the table. 'It was a lovely place.'

'I suppose you didn't want to come back, then?' he asked.

'Oh, yes, I did,' said Rose, standing still and looking at him. 'I'm thankful to be back with you, Frank.'

Her voice shook, but he smiled at her, such a beaming happy smile that we all felt happy too and dragged him to the table, Ellie putting herself next to him as usual.

We felt comfortable and settled, as if the pendulum had swung back into place. We had been away, we had our splendid holiday behind us and now we were back at home, in our accustomed place, with Frank at one end of the table and Rose, looking entirely like her old self now Frank was here, pouring out tea at the other.

We all talked at once, trying to tell Frank everything. The

boys were voluble about their Adventure League and what they had obliged themselves to do for it. Ellie couldn't get in all she wanted to say, so she climbed on Frank's knee to engage his attention. Rose had just cut the sponge cake.

'Did you get my postcard?' I said, leaning over to pull at Frank's sleeve.

'Oh, yes, I did. Thanks very much indeed,' said Frank.

'Mr Salter gave us sixpence, so I bought the stamp and everything,' I said, wishing him to realise the extent of my affection for him.

'Who's Mr Salter?' said Frank.

'Mr Salter was a man what was staying at Bay View,' said Ellie kindly. 'He had a little sitting-room next to ours and in the night he used to come into our room and kneel by Rose's bed, didn't he, Rose?'

Rose jumped to her feet, the cake knife clattering to the floor. A tide of red rushed over her neck and face as she stared at Ellie in horror. Then she picked up the knife and sat down.

'She must have been dreaming,' she said, trying to laugh. She had gone very white now.

'Oh, no,' said Ellie, shaking her curls. 'I wasn't dreaming, because we saw him many a time, didn't we, Diddy?'

When their eyes turned to me, I couldn't bear it. There was something in their faces that frightened me. In the silence, I got down from my chair and pulled Ellie from Frank's knee. Together we rushed out of the room. We rushed to our mother.

'Oh, Mother,' I cried, bursting into the drawing-room where she was having tea with father. 'Ellie's told Frank about

Mr Salter coming into our room in the night and kneeling by Rose's bed and Frank doesn't like it.'

'*What?*' cried my mother in a loud voice, looking so strange, looking like Frank.

My father, too.

I faltered as I repeated it. We were frightened again. We would have run away again, but this time there was nowhere to run to. We had to stand there and be questioned sternly, inexorably. Bewildered, we wept. We gathered that Rose had done something wicked, and that we were wicked too because we hadn't told our parents.

'Why didn't you tell me?' my mother kept saying. 'Why didn't you?'

'Didn't you realise you ought to tell your mother?' said Father. We wept.

'Did Rose tell you not to tell us?' he said.

'Oh, no, no,' I sobbed. 'She didn't tell us anything.'

'Did she know that you knew?' he asked.

'I don't know, I don't know.'

'Did you speak of it to Rose?'

We shook our heads. Our parents stared at us as if we were the most unnatural of children, and in the silence we heard Frank's big feet crunching the gravel on the path round the side of the house. He was going away. He never came back again.

'Poor Frank!' said my mother.

'You two stay down here. I'll send the boys,' she said. 'You're not to go near Rose again.'

She herself went up to the nursery. Years later she told

us it was not she who sent Rose away. Rose went of her own accord that same evening. We never heard of her again. We didn't have another nursemaid. Rose was the last and the best, and the one we have never forgotten.

SATURDAY AFTERNOON

George Thorpe had always gone out on Saturday afternoon. His wife and his daughter Muriel expected him to go out – to go to his club, or play golf or watch cricket matches, or whatever it was he did. When he went, they didn't ask where he was going, and when he came back, they didn't ask where he had been. They were comfortably indifferent to what George did, so long as he got out of the way. They liked the afternoon to themselves on Saturday; they liked to settle down in the sitting-room or the garden, according to the weather, and knit and read and eat chocolates in peace.

Lately, however, George had shown a disinclination to go out, and they'd had to get him out in spite of himself.

'You'd better put your coat on today, George,' said Mrs Thorpe at lunch one chilly Saturday.

'I didn't think of going out, said George, looking at the grey sky.

But after lunch Muriel brought his coat. She and her mother helped him into it and gave him his hat and kissed him.

'Enjoy yourself,' said Mrs Thorpe, as she always did, and when he had gone, Muriel slewed the sofa round to the sitting-room fire for her mother and drew up an armchair for herself.

They looked at George going down the drive – a familiar figure, stooping against the east wind, the fingers of one long, thin hand spread over the crown of his hat to keep it on.

'I don't know what's happened to him,' said Muriel. 'He seems to want to stay at home now on Saturday afternoons.'

'Well, he's not going to,' said Mrs Thorpe, putting her feet up on the sofa. 'Men should go out on Saturday afternoons, after they've been in their offices all week. He'd do nothing but fidget if he stayed in. He must keep up his interests.'

'Oh, I'm all for it,' said Muriel, opening a box of chocolates, although the lunch they had just finished had been hearty. 'Have one?'

'Thanks,' said her mother.

'I suppose he's feeling a bit old,' said Muriel.

'Old!' said Mrs Thorpe indignantly. 'He's the same age as I am, which is fifty-four. I don't feel old, and what's more I don't think I look it.'

'Oh, you!' said Muriel with affectionate banter. 'You're one of the world's wonders.'

They were great friends – two strapping women, as alike as two peas, except that Muriel was the much younger pea, being half the age of her mother. Both had ginger hair, light eyelashes, solid ankles, and good teeth often fully exposed in laughter. They chivied and chipped each other with the greatest good humour. It was fun to come across them in the town, where they would stand laughing and talking to their friends, with always some tale to tell against each other or poor old George. They made George sound quite funny, though no one else found him so – a quiet, self-effacing man who seemed to live only to provide his wife and daughter with plenty of the best of everything.

In the sitting-room this afternoon, Mrs Thorpe and Muriel were very comfortable. The novel soon slipped from Mrs Thorpe's hand; she dozed. Muriel didn't doze, at her age. She read, a hand going out now and again to the chocolates. The fire flapped softly. On the mantelpiece the clock ticked time away. It ticked to half-past three without notice.

'Bother!' said Muriel suddenly, lifting her head from her book. 'There's a man coming up the drive.'

Mrs Thorpe frowned without opening her eyes. 'A man?' she said. 'What ever for?'

'I don't know,' said Muriel. 'But I suppose I shall have to go and see.'

She pulled herself out of the deep chair, tugged at her creased skirt and went out of the room. Mrs Thorpe had almost dozed off again by the time she came back.

'Mother' said Muriel, 'the man wants to see Father. He says he's a police inspector.'

'Of course he isn't,' said Mrs Thorpe, opening her eyes. 'Don't be taken in by *that*.'

'He's an inspector all right,' said Muriel, 'he showed me a silver badge thing inside his coat.'

'What does he want your father for?'

'He didn't say. He says he'll wait until he comes back. He says he'll walk about the garden, so I've let him.'

'Well, he'll be walking about for hours,' said Mrs Thorpe, punching up the sofa cushions and rearranging herself. 'But that's his lookout.'

'Yes, it is,' said Muriel, taking up her book and another chocolate.

They meant to settle back into comfort, but they couldn't. Although Mrs Thorpe closed her eyes and Muriel had hers on her book, both of them were conscious that something kept moving outside the windows. A homburg hat appeared around the rhododendrons, or crossed the lawn, and passed down the drive, only to reappear around the rhododendrons. 'Oh, drat that man!' said Mrs Thorpe, in the end. She heaved her legs to the floor and sat up. 'It's no good trying to rest with him walking about the garden. It's getting on my nerves. What does he want with your father?'

'I haven't any idea,' said Muriel. 'It'll be nothing much. Car licence, or something at the office.'

'Well, early though it is, let's have tea,' said Mrs Thorpe. 'I feel I could do with a cup.'

'All right,' said Muriel, going out to put the kettle on.

But when she came back with the tea tray, and sandwiches, scones and cakes, they still could not forget the man in the garden. No sooner had they settled to tea than there was a scatter of rain on the windows, and in a moment a heavy shower was falling. 'Drat that man!' said Mrs Thorpe again. 'Now we shall have to ask him in. Go and fetch him, Muriel,' she said with resignation. 'Bring him in here, we'll have to give him a cup of tea.'

'No need to bring him in here,' said Muriel, getting up once more. 'He could have it in the kitchen.'

'No. Bring him in here,' said Mrs Thorpe. 'Then I can find out what he's come for.'

Mrs Thorpe sighed for her Saturday afternoon as she watched Muriel, in the drive, gesticulating at the man, who had taken refuge among the rhododendrons. In a moment, Muriel brought him in through the sitting-room door – a tall, solid man who needed no silver badge to proclaim himself a policeman.

'Good afternoon,' said Mrs Thorpe with dignity. (He ought to realise what an interruption he was.) 'You can't wait out there in this rain. You'd better sit down and have a cup of tea.'

'Thank you, madam,' said the man stiffly, 'but that's not necessary. I'm on duty.'

'There's nothing in the regulations about not having tea, I suppose,' said Mrs Thorpe more amiably.

'No, madam.'

'Sit down, then,' said Mrs Thorpe, pouring tea.

The man looked as if he would rather not, but he took an upright chair near the door and put his hat beneath it. Then he waited with a corrugated brow for Muriel to bring tea to him. 'Sandwich?' asked Muriel.

The man hesitated, then took one and put it on his saucer.

'Well?' said Mrs Thorpe, settling back against the cushions and stirring her tea. 'And what is it you want to see my husband about?'

The Inspector coughed. 'I'd rather wait till he comes,' he said.

'Oh, nonsense,' said Mrs Thorpe easily. 'He might be another two hours. You can't sit there saying nothing for all that time. What is it? Is it something to do with the office? Has there been a burglary or something?'

'No,' said the Inspector. 'Nothing of that kind.' He put the whole small sandwich into his mouth at once and chewed stolidly, without looking at her.

'There's no need for all this mystery,' said Mrs Thorpe, helping herself to another sandwich. She always made a good tea. 'If you can tell Mr Thorpe, you can tell me. I'm his wife. I shall know sooner or later, shan't I? So what is it?'

The Inspector looked more uncomfortable than ever. Muriel offered sandwiches, but he shook his head.

'Do,' invited Muriel.

He shook his head again. 'It's this way, Madam,' he said, looking straight at Mrs Thorpe with light, clear eyes. 'I don't think I'd be so welcome if you knew what I've come about.'

'Oh?' said Mrs Thorpe with interest. 'Well, I can't think of anything that would make me grudge you a cup of tea and a sandwich, so help yourself and get this business off your chest.'

'Very well, Madam, if you will have it,' said the man, taking another sandwich as if the consequences must be on her own head now. But still he didn't tell her.

'Come along, man,' said Mrs Thorpe. 'For goodness sake!'

'I'd sooner not in front of the young lady,' the Inspector said.

Mother and daughter burst out laughing. 'You don't need to mind about *me*,' Muriel assured him. 'After all, I'm a big girl now.'

'You're making me downright curious,' said Mrs Thorpe taking a scone. 'Come along now. Out with it.'

'Well,' said the Inspector, coughing again, 'it's about Miss

Foxhall.' He glanced swiftly at Mrs Thorpe, as if this must startle her.

'And who's Miss Foxhall?' said Mrs Thorpe, unstartled.

'You've never heard of her?'

Biting into the crumby scone, Mrs Thorpe shook her head.

'Miss Foxhall was a friend of your husband's,' said the Inspector.

'My husband must know a lot of people I don't know,' said Mrs Thorpe. 'And vice versa. But what's so particular about this Miss Foxhall?'

'She's dead,' said the man.

'Poor thing,' said Mrs Thorpe, unmoved. 'But what's that to us?'

'She was found dead about an hour ago. There was a letter to your husband beside her.'

'A letter to my husband?' repeated Mrs Thorpe. 'Did she want him to do something for her?'

'Not exactly that,' said the Inspector. He wished this woman would give him a little help.

'How old was this Miss Foxhall?' asked Muriel, coming to him with the scones.

He shook his head. If they could eat, he couldn't. He didn't relish jobs of this kind. 'She was about forty-two,' he said.

'Why did she kill herself?' asked Mrs Thorpe.

The Inspector drew in his breath. 'Well, as a matter of fact,' he said, debarrassing himself of his cup and saucer by putting them on top of the bookcase, 'your husband had been a friend of hers for a long time, but a week or two ago he broke with her, it seems – and, well, there you are,' he said, turning his hands out.

There was a silence in the room, while mother and daughter stared at him. 'Broke with her?' said Mrs Thorpe.

'Yes, Madam,' said the Inspector.

There was another silence, except for the gusts of rain against the windows.

'Are you trying to tell me,' said Mrs Thorpe, leaning forward, 'that my husband, George Thorpe, had been living with this woman?'

'I'm just stating the facts, Madam.'

'Facts?' said Mrs Thorpe loudly. 'I never heard anything so silly in all my life. Have you, Muriel? Your father living with a woman and her killing herself because he'd broken with her?'

'Never!' said Muriel vehemently. 'I've never heard such rubbish in my life.'

They turned their flushed, angry faces on the Inspector. He said nothing.

'What on earth do you mean by this tale?' demanded Mrs Thorpe.

He looked at her gravely. 'I'm sorry,' he said. 'But it's true.'

His tone carried conviction. They began to believe him. The colour ebbed slowly from their faces. Mrs Thorpe put down her cup and saucer with a sudden clatter, and Muriel went quickly to her.

'Mother!' she said, but Mrs Thorpe thrust her aside, so that she could look at the Inspector.

'How long had this been going on?' she asked.

'About fifteen years, I should think,' he said.

'Fifteen years!' cried Mrs Thorpe. 'Fifteen years?'

'Well, we've known of it for about that time,' he said.

'You've *known* of it?' she echoed again.

'The police do know these things,' the Inspector said apologetically. 'You see, he'd set her up in a house. At the other end of the town.'

'Oh! A house! A house, Muriel!' cried Mrs Thorpe distractedly. She reached up and clasped Muriel's arm. 'Fifteen years in a house with a woman, and we never dreamed of it! Muriel, can you credit it? George – your father – so quiet, with no life in him at all. Not for *us*, anyhow. And she's killed herself for him –'

'Look,' said Muriel, pointing to the window. 'He's coming back.'

Mrs Thorpe got to her feet and they stared at him, the one who had gone away a few hours earlier so familiar, coming back a stranger. They had never known him, and yet they had gone through him so often, like an old suit, so sure there was nothing in any of the pockets. And for fifteen years he had been living a life they knew nothing of, finding love somewhere else, and was involved now in tragedy and scandal, dragging them into it, too. They watched him come up the drive, holding his hat on, and when he was out of sight, their eyes turned to the door of the room.

He came in, chafing his hands. 'I stopped out as long as I could, but I couldn't stand this wind any longer,' he said, and added with quiet bitterness, 'Sorry to spoil your afternoon.'

Then he saw the Inspector.

COVER

When Harry Smith married Meg Saunders everybody thought it was very good of him. He thought it was good of him too. Coming down the aisle of the village church with the shrinking Meg on his arm, he squared his shoulders in the sight of the thronged pews. He had always liked to do the admired thing, and this time he felt he had excelled himself.

It wasn't every man, coming back from the war, would marry the girl who had jilted him for an American airman and actually had a baby. But Harry Smith had created a standard for himself in the village. He had something to live up to.

Everybody liked him, or almost everybody, and he liked to be liked. He had made himself liked not only down at the pub and in the cottages, but at the Vicarage and the Hall. He was looked upon as their right-hand man by both the Vicar and the Squire in all the activities those active gentlemen promoted for the good of the village.

Nobody expected Harry Smith to forgive Meg, and when he not only forgave her but re-engaged himself to her it made a great stir.

But, to his eye, what she had done in his absence hadn't made much outward difference to Meg. She was as pretty as ever, though quieter, and after all the man had been killed and the baby had died as soon as it was born. So Harry was willing to let bygones be bygones, not quite so far as Meg was concerned, but so far as he himself was concerned. The village marvelled at this magnanimity and he enjoyed his situation.

Besides, it was a bit awkward for him with an ailing father on his hands. He had to cycle into the nearby town every day to his work and the old man couldn't be left alone.

When he asked Meg to marry him, she cried for a long time and said she couldn't. But he persisted and she was glad to give in at last. She had been so cut off from everybody since the affair with Johnny Crowe.

Everybody in the village had thought badly of Meg, but none so badly as Meg herself. She was not the only girl to succumb to an American. The aerodrome had been so near that it had ruined not only the village by macadamising its fields for miles around, but it ruined many of the girls. But everybody considered, and so did Meg, that she, the school-master's daughter, should have known better.

She was crushed by what happened to her. When she hadn't heard from Johnny Crowe for a long time she timidly waylaid one of the men from the aerodrome and asked for news.

'Why, that guy was shot down weeks ago,' said the man, staring at her.

'Oh, thank you,' said Meg, backing away.

'Yes, with Larry James and Glen Sternberg and that lot . . . '

'Oh!' said Meg, backing still farther. All she wanted was to get away, to run, to hide . . .

She found a place for herself in London. The baby died the day it was born, and when she was better she had to come home to nurse her father. It was a dreadful ordeal to return to the village. She had been brought up to set an example. Her father was a priggish man and she felt she had brought him down. She felt she was a disgrace to him, to herself and the whole community. She dared not make any attempt to re-enter the social life of the village and was always alone, until Harry Smith came back.

Then he changed everything. She didn't feel for him what she had felt for Johnny Crowe, but she didn't want to. Never such heartrending love again, she said to herself. It was too much. She didn't even let her thoughts return to that terrible year.

But she had liked Harry before she saw Johnny Crowe; and she was young. She had been desperately unhappy and now happiness seemed within reach again – the blessed, ordinary happiness of a place in life, of having a home and a man to look after, the happiness of being allowed at last to sink into the general inconspicuousness, instead of being singled out and kept apart. It was Harry who offered all this, and from his offer a new devotion was born. She loved him because he had forgiven and reinstated her.

He insisted on being married in the village church, though Meg had hoped to be allowed to slip away to the register-office in the town. Not only did she feel it wasn't fitting she should be married in a church, she dreaded all the eyes she knew would come and stare at her. But Harry said he wasn't going to sneak away to his own wedding.

'I'm not going to act as if I'm ashamed of marrying you,' he said, and though she winced from the publicity she thought he was wonderful.

As a matter of fact, he wasn't ashamed at all; he was proud of himself. So he made as much of the occasion as possible and Meg got through it as best she could and they went to live with his father.

When, after a few months, the old man died, the Squire made an offer to Harry. The Squire, in his turn, was beset by the problem that had been Harry's; he had to find someone to look after an ageing parent. In both cases Meg was the unconscious answer. The Squire suggested that Harry and Meg should have board and lodging in his mother's big house in the town and that in return Meg should look after the old lady.

Harry jumped at the offer. He was tired of the village. The sensation he had made in coming back from the war and marrying Meg had died away and things were very quiet. He welcomed the idea of making new acquaintances, of being liked by a larger circle. So, with much talk of being glad to oblige the Squire, of the Squire's having been such a good friend to him that he was glad to do something in return and so on, they moved.

Meg was glad to leave the village for the town. This was really to be the fresh start she had hoped for when she married Harry. Somehow the marriage alone had not been that. But now at last she was getting away from the place where everybody knew. The town might be only four miles away, but it was a town and there were a lot of people in it; few, if any, could have heard of her or her story.

Everything started well. The Squire's mother, Mrs Castle, proved to be a nice old lady, if remote and determined to discourage conversation. The house was an ancient manor-house now engulfed by the town's shopping centre. During the day the tops of the green buses slid past the high garden wall, and from the upper windows as she worked Meg could see women going in and out of the shops, men going in and out of offices and children rushing home from school and back again.

At night and on Sundays, when the shops were closed and the owners gone to their homes, it was very quiet round the manor-house, quieter than in any village. Harry, who took to the town like a duck to water, was out almost every night, and it would have been lonely for Meg if she hadn't, almost at once, discovered Ivy.

Ivy was a stranger to the town too, but she had come from London. Her father had married again and she didn't like his wife, so she had come to live with her aunt, Mrs Mobbs, and help in the shop, where they sold cigarettes, newspapers, flypapers, paper patterns, jam-pot covers and small toys. Ivy was eighteen and pretty, with long lashes and blonde curls. She was always laughing and was far too popular in the shop for her aunt's peace of mind.

'I wish I'd gone in for a wool-shop,' said Mrs Mobbs to Meg, after she had been in two or three times. 'Or ladies' underwear, and then the men wouldn't be able to come in. But with selling cigarettes, they've got the excuse. No good putting 'Sorry, no cigs.' on the door, they come in just the same and say they thought I didn't mean it. Yes, I wish I'd gone in for wool.'

'Oh, go on, Aunty,' said Ivy, with a laugh. 'As if I'd have come if you had.'

On summer evenings when Harry had gone to play darts in one bar or another, Meg took Mrs Castle's old dog for a walk in the public gardens by the bus terminus and back, and by and by Ivy began to go with her.

'My mind's at rest when she's with you,' said Mrs Mobbs.

Meg was happy to have a friend; she hadn't had a girl for a friend for years. She mostly let Ivy do the talking. There was so much she couldn't talk about herself. But she listened to Ivy and took great pleasure in Ivy's looks and prospects in life, and she was as careful of her as was Mrs Mobbs herself. At the bus stop she always knew which bus-conductor must be left severely alone and which one it was safe to exchange back-chat with. She stood smilingly by while Ivy bickered, taking no part herself, but indulgently letting Ivy play.

She talked so glowingly about her new friend to Harry that he said he'd better go into the shop and see for himself.

'Oh, do, you're sure to like her,' said Meg, warmly.

He went. He introduced himself as Meg's husband, and Mrs Mobbs said she was pleased to meet him. Ivy laughed and gave him twenty cigarettes from under the counter.

Harry secretly considered Ivy a smasher, though when he went home he responded but coolly to Meg's eager 'Well?'

'Yes, she seems a nice girl all right,' he said. 'Why don't you invite her to tea on Sunday?'

It must be admitted that Harry took the trouble to make it look as if it was for someone else's good that he was doing what he wanted. Some people do not bother to do that. But Harry did.

'Ask her to tea on Sunday,' he said.

'Oh, I don't know if Mrs Castle . . .'

'Rubbish,' said Harry. 'Nothing was said about us not being able to have our friends in.'

Our friends. It sounded wonderful to Meg. Quite like other people, other young married couples. She approached Mrs Castle, who, being of the old school still even in these days, gave permission on condition that there was not too much noise.

Meg flew down the street to give the invitation to both Ivy and Mrs Mobbs. But Mrs Mobbs asked to be excused, she said she'd rather have a lie down. The shop kept her up all through the week she said, but she always felt a bit tired on Sundays. Ivy could go with pleasure, she said, and Ivy said 'Thanks ever so.' Meg flew home, full of plans for Sunday's tea. She was a great cook and it was an excitement to have her friend to cook for.

When Ivy arrived, achieving a very London effect with her curls and a pleated skirt flying out from her slim legs, the table was spread with cakes and biscuits, buns, sandwiches and tarts in her honour, and Meg, flushed with the novelty of her situation, took her place behind the teapot.

It was a lively party. Harry laid himself out to amuse the guest, and Ivy laughed so much that old Mrs Castle, far away behind her portières and thick doors, frowned at what things had come to.

When tea was over they all went for a walk, and when that

was over Harry saw Ivy home because it was dark, while Meg did the washing up.

Harry fell into the way of dropping into the shop once a day, sometimes oftener. Ivy liked him – who didn't? Mrs Mobbs liked him too, at first. Ivy didn't go out with the dog in the evenings now. She said it was too hot. But she walked up to the manor-house and sat in the kitchen with Meg and Harry instead, and when it got late and she said she must be going, Harry took her home as a matter of course.

Meg was quite unsuspicious, but Mrs Mobbs wasn't. Harry was too fond of leaning on the counter, staring at Ivy, for her liking. And she wasn't sure that Ivy wasn't attracted either. But the girl had teased her so about previous, unfounded suspicions that Mrs Mobbs was uncertain of herself. Modern goings-on bewildered her so much that she often said to herself she didn't know *what* to think.

But one hot noon she caught sight of Harry in the town. From one shifty glance of his eyes she knew he had seen her and was hoping she hadn't seen him. Anybody would be justified, Mrs Mobbs thought, in distrusting a man who looked like that.

She walked in at one door of a store and straight out of another. Harry was just disappearing up the street her shop was in. She followed him. She went in the back way and came into the shop in time to catch Harry kissing Ivy behind the door.

'I thought as much,' said Mrs Mobbs, very red in the face from heat and emotion.

There was a dead silence. The protagonists stared at one another.

'You'll get out of this shop, Harry Smith,' said Mrs Mobbs getting her breath back. 'And you'll not set foot in it again. If ever you do, I'll go to see your employer.'

'Nay, come, Mrs Mobbs,' said Harry, trying to laugh it off. 'It's not so serious as all that, surely. What's a kiss in these days?'

'I don't know what it is to men like you,' said Mrs Mobbs. 'But I'm not discussing it. You get out and stop out, I've told you.'

'Just as you say,' said Harry lightly. He tried to saunter out with nonchalance, but he looked a fool.

'Ivy,' said Mrs Mobbs to the girl, who was trying without success to look indignant with her aunt instead of deeply ashamed of herself. 'I don't know how you could do it,' said Mrs Mobbs sternly. 'That man's married and what's more, he's married to your friend.'

That went home. Ivy raised her eyes to her aunt and they showed full of tears. Her lip trembled.

'If you ever speak to that Smith again, you go back to London,' went on Mrs Mobbs. 'I stand in the relation of a mother to you, my girl, and I'm going to look after you whether you like it or not. I'm ashamed of you, but I'm not going to keep on about it. You can go up and clean your room out this afternoon. I'd rather not have you about me today. I'm too upset.'

Hanging her head, Ivy went upstairs in silence.

Towards the end of the afternoon Meg dashed rather breathlessly into the shop.

'Oh, Mrs Mobbs, isn't it hot? I've just run down to tell Ivy to be sure to come up tonight. I've made some ice-cream. Where is she, Mrs Mobbs? Is she out?'

Mrs Mobbs rose heavily from her stool behind the counter.

'No, Mrs Smith,' she said. 'Ivy's not out, she's upstairs.'

'Oh, I'll go up, shall I?'

'I'd rather you didn't, Mrs Smith, thank you,' said Mrs Mobbs, ponderously. She didn't like her situation. She wasn't going to say anything to this young woman about her husband if she could help it.

Meg stared at her.

'Is – is anything wrong?' she faltered.

'Ivy can't come to your house any more, Mrs Smith. I'm sorry,' said Mrs Mobbs.

In the light shining whitely up from the papers on the counter, Meg's eyes were dark in her young face. She stood without moving, looking at Mrs Mobbs. Then she turned away and went out of the shop.

'Poor young thing, she knows why,' said Mrs Mobbs, sitting heavily down again. 'She must have had the same trouble with him before.'

Meg went home. She came into the kitchen where Harry was reading the paper at the table. He guessed where she had been. She stood beside him so long in silence that he had to make a move at last.

'Aren't we going to have any tea today?' he said.

'Harry,' said Meg in a low voice.

'Well?' he said after a moment, since she did not go on.

'Mrs Mobbs says Ivy can't come here any more.'

His hands tightened on the paper. His eyes moved sideways, waiting.

'I suppose,' said Meg slowly, 'it's because she's heard about me.'

He relaxed. He stretched out his legs and turned the paper round.

'Yes,' he said. 'I suppose that's it.'

If you have enjoyed this Persephone book why not telephone or write to us for a free copy of the Persephone Catalogue and the current Persephone Biannually? All Persephone books ordered from us cost £10 or three for £27 plus £2 postage per book.

PERSEPHONE BOOKS LTD
59 Lamb's Conduit Street
London WC1N 3NB

Telephone: 020 7242 9292
Fax: 020 7242 9272
sales@persephonebooks.co.uk
www.persephonebooks.co.uk

Persephone Books publishes forgotten fiction and
non-fiction by unjustly neglected authors. The following
titles are available: